D0331899

JiGGY THE
VAMPiRESLAYER

Don't miss the original Jiggy McCue series!

The Killer Underpants
The Toilet of Doom
The Meanest Genie
The Snottle
The Curse of the Poltergoose
Nudie Dudie
Neville the Devil
Ryan's Brain
The Iron, the Switch and the Broom Cupboard
Kid Swap
One for All and All for Lunch
Rudie Dudie

Visit Michael Lawrence's website:
www.wordybug.com

And find loads of Jiggy fun at:
www.jiggymccue.com

JIGGY THE VAMPIRE SLAYER

MICHAEL LAWRENCE

ORCHARD

ORCHARD BOOKS
338 Euston Road, London NW1 3BH
Orchard Books Australia
Level 17/207 Kent Street, Sydney, NSW 2000

First published in the UK in 2011

ISBN 978 1 40830 804 2

Text © Michael Lawrence 2011
Cover illustration © Steve May 2011

A CIP catalogue record for this book is available from the British Library.

3 5 7 9 10 8 6 4 2

Orchard Books is a division of Hachette Children's Books,
an Hachette UK company.

www.hachette.co.uk

This book is dedicated to
Matt Reed,
who has been on the receiving end of a bat...

Some family trees have beautiful leaves,
and some have a bunch of nuts. It is the nuts
that make the tree worth shaking.
Anon

INTRODUCTION BY Jiggy McCue

I never liked history. History should stay where it belongs, I always say. (That's the past, in case you wonder.) Most of the historical rubbish in my school life has been taught by Mr Hurley, whose personal mission is obviously to bore the pants and knickers off everyone in his class. And it works. Some of us, including me, can hardly keep awake in his lessons. So thanks to Mr H I'd given history the big elbow. No more of that pre-Jiggy junk for me, I thought.

But then two things happened.

Thing 1. Hurley-Burley got himself a sabbatical (lengthy skive) working on a cruise ship in the Mediterroonean. We put out the balloons and flags, imagining three history-free months of joy. Should have known better. The dictators who run Ranting Lane School don't do joy.

Thing 2. We got a new history teacher.

The new teacher was called Mr Worzel, and he was as much like Mr Hurley as Hurley is to a sherbet dip. Mr H is past his prime by about three centuries, but always smart in a prehistoric sort of way. Mr Worzel looked at least half Hurley's age and was as scruffy as anyone can be who doesn't spend his nights dozing among cardboard boxes under a bridge. All he needed was straw in his ears and a pole (small 'p') to horizonate his arms and he'd have looked like something you put in a field to frighten crows. He wasn't frightening to us kids, though. His lips looked like they wanted to break into an ear-to-ear almost all the time, and – hard to believe, him being a teacher and all – he actually seemed to *like* talking to us. But he was only a temp. Just filling the happy vacuum left by Hurley while H steamed round the Med sending passengers into a coma with the history of the places they docked at. Temp or not, I was so against any more history by the time Mr W turned up that I resisted him totally – until the day I corrected him.

'Sir,' I said from my usual position at the back of the class.

'Dave,' he said from his usual position at the front.

'Jiggy,' I said.

'What?' he said.

'My name,' I said.

'I meant mine,' he said.

'Your what?' I said.

'Name,' he said.

'Don't get you,' I said.

'Dave,' he said.

'No, you're Worzel,' I said. 'Mister,' I said.

'Dave too,' he said.

'You are?' I said.

'Yes,' he said. 'It's what I told you to call me, don't you remember?'

'When?' I said.

'The day I joined you,' he said.

'Can't have been listening that day,' I said.

'Anyway, what was it you wanted?' he said.

'When?' I said.

'Just now,' he said. 'When you said "Sir", and this fascinating conversation started.'

'I forget,' I said.

But then I remembered.

'No, wait,' I said. 'Got it.'

'Go on then,' he said.

'Well,' I said.

And that's when I set him straight. He'd been warbling about life in the Middle Ages and had uttered something I knew wasn't right. It doesn't matter what, too yawnworthy to go over it again, but the amazing thing is that he wasn't annoyed that I'd questioned his words. Hurley would have blown a neck valve, but Mr Worzel said he'd check on it and get back to me. He sounded quite pleased with me actually. Maybe because I'd been paying attention for a change.

Someone who wasn't pleased was Pete Garrett, who sits next to me. 'What is *wrong* with you, McCue?' he hissed.

'Whajamean?' I whispered back, wiping Garrett spit out of my ear.

'You just had a serious conversation with a teacher. A *history* teacher! We don't *do* that – we're boys.'

'I know,' I said, deeply ashamed. 'It just sort of slipped out.'

'What are you doing knowing stuff like that

anyway?' he demanded.

The time had come to deny everything. 'I didn't know it,' I whispered. 'I was just poking him with a stick to see if he'd twitch. Pete, it's history. What do I know about history? What do I care?'

'You two at the back,' Mr Worzel said. 'You will let me know when you've finished, won't you?'

'Will do, Dave,' I said.

Pete wasn't done yet in any case.

'Listen,' he said – to me, not Dave. 'Our job is to keep our heads down. Get through this school life-sentence without being noticed too much. Keep pulling stunts like that and you'll be escorted off the premises. Either that or end up a prefect. Exclusion from us masses either way. And you want to watch out for that one.'

'What one?'

He nodded towards the front, where Mr W was waiting patiently for him to get all this out of his system. 'All that "Call me Dave" schmooze. It's to get you on his side. Get you to like him.'

'And that's a bad thing?' I said.

'Of course it's a bad thing. Jig, he's a teacher. A *teacher*!'

'OK, I'll try and remember that.' I gave Mr W the thumb. 'We're done.'

'Thank you,' he said. 'Now where were we?'

'Classroom,' I said. 'RLSTB.'

'RLSTB?'

'Ranting Lane Sanatorium for the Terminally Braindead.'

'Oh, yes,' he said, and shot back to the Middle Ages without a Tardis.

Fortunately for my eardrums, Pete wasn't once again in my pocket when Mr W approached me next day in the playground.

'It pains me to say it, Jiggy,' he said, 'but you were right. I was talking out of my sporran.'

'Didn't know you were Scottish, sir,' I said.

'Dave. And I'm not.'

'Not Dave?'

'Scottish. Don't do it again, eh?'

'Do what again?'

'Correct me in class. Please? Makes me look a right dumbo.'

'Make sure you get it right next time then.'

'I'll try.'

He winked, and strolled off.

What no one knew – this would have sent Pete into an instant nosedive off a cliff – was that I hadn't been hazarding a wild guess when I corrected Dave W in class. I'd been doing research into Medieval times, you see. Why? Because of a recent birthday pres from the aged parents. A phoney antique scroll produced by a company that claimed to be able to find ancestors who share a person's DNA to the last follicle and wart. Apparently, all that these geezers needed to identify your long-dead relatives was a swab of saliva, and my treacherous mother had tiptoed into my room one night, lifted a mouthful of mine while I snoozed, and handed it over to them. Then, armed with my mouth juice, the firm's computers started tracking back through the years looking for Jiggy doubles, and lo, they found one in fourteen hundred and something.*

Fine, you'd think. You might even think fun. But my birthday scroll told me hardly anything about this reverse Jiggy clone, only that he hung with knights of the armoured kind. There was so little info that my first thought was 'So what?', but over the next couple of days (and knights) I got to

---

* To hear more of this, see the first Jiggy's Genes book: *Jiggy's Magic Balls*. (The DNA research company, by the way, was called Genetic Investigations in Time, or GIT.)

wondering what sort of life someone like me might have lived in those days, and I looked up the period, first with search engines, then in actual books, at the library. Now no boy in my class ever admits to going to the library, so I had to sneak in and out in my father's safari hat from Help the Aged. I was still spotted, though, and who by? Well, of course! Bryan Ryan, archest of all my enemies. Ryan, naturally, made some stupid comment about jelly-heads who spend time in libraries, and I, naturally, thumped him, and he, naturally, thumped me back, and we went our separate unmerry ways shouting threats to prepare for the next time we met.

Anyway, that's how I learnt about life in the Middle Ages and was able to correct Dave Worzel. But after what Pete said in class I vowed to turn my back on history forever, and I would have too if I hadn't forgotten that the Golden Oldies had signed a contract with the ancestral research bods for not one but *three* DNA runs on previous Jiggy types. I only remembered this when I got in from school the day after I put DW right and saw, on the kitchen table, another big envelope with my name on the label and GIT in the corner.

I hesitated before opening the envelope. Did I really want to know about someone else who looked like me, thought like me, maybe had the same taste in underpants as me?

No.

Absolutely not.

I opened the envelope.

The scroll inside was exactly like the first one except that it mentioned a different Jiggy. No surprise there. What was a surprise was how recent this one was. Well, not *that* recent. He pre-dated my great-grandparents, but I'd seen old black-and-white newsreels of his time, so it felt a bit of a cheat. Even though he wasn't from really way back, though, there wasn't a whole lot of guff about him. This is it:

Born 1892-3. Little is known of him other than that he was the only son of tradespeople, but there are indications that he might have been a soldier in adult life. Either that or involved in some sort of blood sport.

Blood sport? I didn't like the sound of that. Soldier was better. I'm not heavily into action films or anything, but I could handle an ancestor who joined the army and wore a uniform and travelled all over, fighting for king and country or whatever, firing rifles and cannons and all. Yes, I reckoned that I...

But then I remembered Pete. How disappointed he'd be if he heard that I'd got interested in some other bit of history. He was probably right anyway. This was century twenty-one. The modern age. Like Garrett, I had better things to do with my life than think about stuff that happened before my block of time. I shoved the scroll back in the envelope and went into the living room. Turned the telly on.

JiGGY THE VAMPiRE SLAYER

AS TOLD BY THE EDWARDIAN JiGGY

CHAPTER ONE

My first names are Jerome Ignatius Granville, but I call myself Jig for short and Jiggy for long, and can you blame me? I wish I could do something about my double-barrelled surname too. The first part of the barrel is my mother's maiden name, Offal, which she pronounces 'Orful' because she's a snob. The second part, my father's family name, is Trype, which I'm sad to say makes us Offal-Trypes. Embarrassing as that can sometimes be, it might not be *so* bad if we were chinless aristocrats, but we're not. Father's a butcher. The sign over his shop reads OFFAL-TRYPE, FAMILY BUTCHER (though no families are butchered on the premises). The three of us live above the shop. It's not a big flat, but Mother makes it as nice as she can without the maid and housekeeper she says a woman of quality should have. She's even nagged Father into installing a bath with plumbing, and a 'Venerable

Thomas Crapper & Company' water closet. Cost him a fortune, all that, and he never stops grumbling about it, but I think he's rather proud of it in a quiet sort of way, especially the lavatory, which he spends far more time flushing than he needs to.

So there you have me, in one big fat nutshell: Jerome Ignatius Granville Offal-Trype, butcher's son, living in a two-bedroom flat over the shop with my parents and a flushable toilet, 1906 anno Domini. And that's the nutshell I would have stayed in if we hadn't visited the zoological gardens one November afternoon, but before I get to that I'd better mention a couple of other things. Such as that Father employed me (for a pittance) to deliver meat to customers who couldn't be bothered to carry it home themselves. I had a black bicycle with a basket on the front and a tin plate on the side bearing the words 'Offal-Trype', and when delivering I had to wear an ankle-length white apron and a straw hat. I know I should have been grateful to have work because a lot of people didn't, but I couldn't bear the look, smell or feel of meat, any meat, any shape or form. I didn't even eat *cooked* meat if I could avoid it. Father knew how I felt and wasn't sympathetic. It upset him that I didn't want to take over from him when he retired. And here's something else. Not only did I have no plans to be a butcher when I grew up, but I didn't have any other plans either. I certainly didn't want to do anything out of the ordinary, or even travel much. I got all the excitement I wanted from the adventure stories of my favourite author, Edric MacIntyre-Quiver – Q to his fans. I just loved Q's stirring tales. Couldn't get enough of them.

The worst of living above a butcher's shop was the stench of dead meat that seeped up through the floorboards. You didn't notice it most of the time you were indoors because you got used to it, but when you went home after being out for a while it really hit you. Hit me anyway, and Mother to some extent. I would groan as I climbed the stairs to the flat while she would pull a face and wave a hanky under her nose. She said the odour clung to her hair and clothes, and to cover it doused herself in a scent that was almost as bad. 'Mother,' I would say, 'that perfume is *killing* my nose nerves,' but she would tell me to put up with it because she wasn't going *anywhere* smelling of dead animals.

And so we come to the big day out that was to ruin my life. Mother made Father and me wear our best clothes for the occasion – he his Sunday suit, me my knickerbockers. We hate dressing up, Father and I, but there's only one boss in our house and it isn't us. Mother put on her best dress (blue), a big hat with feathers, gloves that went up to her elbows, and her fox-fur stole, but stayed inside as long as possible while Father and I waited along the pavement for the tram. 'A lady cannot be seen loitering in the street,' she said in her most toffee-nosed voice. She wasn't a patient waiter, though, and every so often she would lean out and tut loudly about public transport being '*so* unreliable', and get all hoity about everything in sight, such as dog mess, litter, the state of the iron railings beside our front door. (The railings were pointed like spears and in need of a coat of paint, but I'd seen worse.)

There'd been thick swirly fogs for a week and today wasn't much better, so we were glad when the tram finally arrived. 'It's here, dear!' Father called, and Mother stepped off our step and walked like royalty towards the stop. Father, because he knew his place, made a show of handing her up the tram steps and ushering her to her seat, where she arranged herself elegantly and warned us not to sit on the material of her dress.

The 'zoological gardens and menagerie' had only been open a few days, but it looked like being a really popular attraction. I'd never seen so many people flocking to one place on any day of the week, and this was Sunday, the day most people stay at home and do nothing. A lot of the visitors had walked there. Others, like us, had come by tram, or by motor omnibus. A few had journeyed there by horse-drawn carriage, top-hatted driver and all. Those people acted like they owned everything in sight and Mother got as close to them as she could so folk would take her for one of them. 'Ideas above her station,' Father muttered. 'Always did have, your ma.' Mother's father was a shoemaker, but you'd never know it from the way she Lady Mucked all over the place. I once asked Father how the two of them had got together, him being so down-to-earth and plain-speaking and her anything but. He told me that shortly after they met she got it into her head that he would rise above his humble origins and take her with him. 'She thought the shop was just a start,' he said. 'Imagined I'd expand and eventually own a high-class department store like Harrods. No idea where she got that from. Happy with my little meat shop, me.'

There were turnstiles at the entrance to the gardens. Some in the queue were grumbling about the price of entry. 'It'll never catch on if they keep charging this sort of money,' one man said loudly as he steered his family through. There were strange trees and shrubs all over the gardens, and enormous hot-houses stuffed with exotic plants that made me think of Q's jungle adventures, but what most people had come for was the menagerie (already being called 'the zoo' because it was easier).

The menagerie/zoo was amazing. Cages and paddocks full of creatures no one had ever seen before in the flesh. Flamingos, for instance. Flamingos are really weird, all pink, with long curved beaks and legs like bent pencils. The lions and tigers were smaller than I'd expected from paintings and engravings, but the way they prowled about and eyed me through the bars fair took my breath away. And I loved the giraffes, gobbling leaves from the tops of trees, and the *Camelus bactrianus*, loping along with its two big hairy humps and snooty expression. The kangaroos were amusing, too, and I was fascinated by the stripes of the zebras, and there were apes and monkeys − lots of monkeys − and great lumbering hippopotamuses and rhinoceroses, and birds, so many *types* of bird, amazingly coloured, and feathered beasts called ostriches that stalked about as though they were just learning to walk. Mother had been determined not to be impressed by any of this, yet even she fell silent before some creatures, forgetting to complain about the crowds, the animal odours and so forth.

Entrance to almost all of the enclosures was forbidden, but there was one, *The Small Nocturnal Mammals House*, which visitors were permitted to go into. Mother was about to lead the way when Father mentioned that some of the nocturnal mammals would be bats.

'Bats?' Mother said. 'You mean *actual* bats?'

Father fluttered his fingers and hissed through his teeth. 'Yesss…'

She screwed her face up. 'Oh, I don't want to see things like *that*.'

'Thought you might not,' said Father.

'I've never seen a bat,' I said.

'I have,' he said. 'Dark night, it was. Came at me like it wanted to tear me head off.'

'And did it?'

'Yeah, this is a new one.'

I asked if I could go in and he said I could. So while Mother went all shuddery at the thought of the bats, I strolled into *The Small Nocturnal Mammals House* alone. I didn't know it, but this was a mistake. A very big one. If I'd known what my curiosity would lead to I would have taken my chances with the big cats rather than go in there.

CHAPTER TWO

The Small Nocturnal Mammals House was divided into sections and species, but it was the bats I wanted to see, so I went straight to their enclosure. It was so dark in there that my first thought was that someone had forgotten to light the lamps, but then I remembered that bats only come out at night, so they probably never lit the lamps in there. As my eyes got used to the gloom I could just make out rocks and small caves and spindly trees. I also saw that I wasn't the only visitor. A few others stood silently about, presumably waiting for something to happen. When nothing did, they drifted out in ones and twos, leaving me alone there. If there were any bats present, you wouldn't have known it. There were quiet rustlings and flappings and small whistling sounds, but that was it. After a while, I thought, 'Well, so that's bats,' and was about to leave when there was a frantic fluttering and several of them flew out of one of the caves followed by a larger, paler bat whose eyes glowed as piercingly as tiny beams of light. I sank into a crouch to watch all this, but the pursued bats quickly scattered into various holes and the pale one fluttered to a tree near me, landed on a branch, and swung around it to hang upside down by its feet. I remained squatting, not daring to move, and silence descended – silence and absolute stillness – until, all of a sudden, something spurted onto my upturned face. So startled was I by this that I couldn't help but emit a squawk. I still did not dare move, however, so the squawk was succeeded by a pause. I was still pausing when I heard a voice – not with my ears, but inside my head – speaking in a rich foreign accent.

'I am sorry, I did not see you zerre. I sought I voz alone.'

I looked for the source of the voice, and quickly realised – my eyes being sufficiently used to the darkness by now – that the only living thing in the enclosure apart from myself was the small grey creature hanging from the nearby branch: the bat, which was now staring at me with its luminous eyes. My blood ran cold before those bright little dots and I jumped up and ran out of there – right into Mother's arms.

'Jerome, what is it?' she said.* But before I could answer, she flung me out at arm's length. 'What's that on your face?'

'I think a bat urinated on me,' I answered.

'A bat *what*?'

Father, who was also there, chuckled. 'He said a bat peed on him.'

'How disgusting!' cried Mother. Then she pinched her nostrils between thumb and forefinger. 'And what is that *dreadful* odour?'

'I can't smell anything,' I said, and I couldn't, apart from her perfume, which smelt stronger than ever.

'Hector!'

'Yes, dear?'

'Escort Jerome to the tram stop. We must get him home and into the bath!'

She kept her distance while Father walked me out of the zoo and the gardens. I had no complaint about her staying away from me, the way she stank,

---

* Mother was one of the few people who still called me Jerome. My father had been easier to train.

but was puzzled when our fellow passengers on the tram didn't cover their noses near her but did near me. Everyone shrank from me except Father, who'd lost his sense of smell years earlier when a side of beef fell from a hook and broke his hooter.

When we got off at our stop, my nostrils received another nasty blow. I always wince outside the shop, but the smell was so bad now that I had to hold onto the railings by our front door to steady myself. Inside, it was even worse, and upstairs in the flat, where the stink of meat was almost visible, my stomach lurched madly. I only just made it to the water closet.

Ever since Mother persuaded Father to have the latest personal hygiene equipment installed, she'd been obsessed with cleanliness. Not only did she bathe every day, but she forced Father and me to take weekly baths too. Once a week was bad enough, so imagine how happy I was to be ordered into the bath for the second time in five days. But Mother was in one of her defy-me-at-your-peril moods, and I knew better than to go against her at such times.

I'd just stripped down to my birthday suit and donned my dressing gown prior to trudging to the bathroom when I heard an odd noise at my bedroom window and was startled to see a bat throwing itself at the glass. I raised the window to knock it away, but it was too quick for me, and in it came. It was late afternoon and dark already, but I'd lit the lamp by my bed, so I was able to see the creature well enough. It was brown and furry, with membranous wings and a small mean face, and it made a sharp, angry sort of sound as it struck one wall after another before parking itself on the high back of my easy chair. From there it stared at me as though waiting to see what I would do next, but the truth is, I didn't know *what* to do. I had no experience of driving bats from rooms. Perhaps I can persuade it back outside with something, I thought. My cricket bat stood against the wall behind the door. I grabbed it, but as I hefted it the other bat (the winged one) did something extraordinary.

It began to grow and change shape!

In a handful of ticks the creature that had just flown in my window sat not on the back of the chair but in it, and the cold eyes that stared at me were no longer those of a brown bat but a full-grown man in a tweed suit.

'Well now,' the gentleman said, leaning forward, 'don't *you* smell enticing?'

I had no immediate answer to this, but as he rose from the chair I gripped my cricket bat tightly and managed a few words of enquiry.

'Who are you? What trick was that? What do you want?'

My visitor grinned, very broadly, and two sharply pointed teeth grew suddenly from the upper gums at the extremes of his mouth.

'What I *want*,' he said, 'is your blood.'

'My b-blood?'

'Don't worry, it'll only hurt for a minute or two. Three at the outside.'

With his two sharpest teeth hanging over his lower lip, he took a step towards me. I smelt mothballs.

'Now wait a minute,' I said. 'You can't have my blood. I need it.'

'So do I,' he returned. 'It's my teatime.'

I suppose the sensible thing would have been to shout for Mother, who would have raced in and thrown the man downstairs while Father and I stood behind her, cheering. But I didn't think of that. Instead I ran to the window and raised it as far as it would go.

'I think you'd better leave, sir,' I said.

He did not leave but changed direction to advance on me once again. He was a couple of feet away and the panic was rising within me when my arm came up and the cricket bat whacked him on the side of the head. This surprised me as much as him because whacking uninvited visitors with cricket bats had not been part of the education that Mother had insisted upon. He staggered badly, though not as badly as when the bat whacked him a second time, whereupon he lost his balance and tumbled out of the window.

I rushed to the ledge and watched his graceless descent. My bedroom, like all of the rooms above the shop, was just one floor up, so it wasn't far to the pavement; but he didn't even make it that far, landing instead on the railings below. He screamed horribly as their spearlike points pierced him, but it was a short scream, cut off in its prime as his body sort of imploded, and…turned to dust.

CHAPTER THREE

Next morning, entering the dining room, I went to the window to see what sort of day it was, and sighed. Another foggy one. Soon I would be out there, delivering Father's meat. It's no fun riding your bicycle from one foggy address to another. Standing there, I caught a movement below, and could just make out Mother sweeping something into the gutter. Dust, I assumed. From the ferocious way she was doing it I guessed she was having one of her moans about not having servants to clear the mess left by the lower orders who pass our door.

I went to the sideboard and ladled porridge into a bowl. Father has sausage, bacon, kidneys, chops and other meaty things for breakfast. Not me. Mother's porridge is always lumpy, but at least it doesn't contain the blood and bits of dead animals. The fire hadn't yet been lit and I shivered as I sat to gulp the lumpy grey stuff. I hadn't slept much last night, maybe because I wasn't used to tweedy gentlemen entering my room as bats and informing me that they want my blood. I was still thinking about my visitor and what had happened to him when I was startled by a commotion in the chimney breast and a flurry of winged creatures flew out, scattering soot.

More bats!

The sight of them was enough for me to abandon my porridge bowl (but not my spoon) and slide under the table. It wasn't much of a hiding place. The tablecloth, though it fell on all sides, ended halfway to the floor. As I cowered there, six pairs of shoes, with feet in them and legs above them, appeared in the space between the carpet and the cloth. Four of the pairs stood at the table's long sides and two at its narrower ends. Eight of the shoes were gentlemen's. The other four were ladies'.

'Get him!'

'Haul him out!'

'Drain him!'

Though these words were spoken by just three of my visitors, all six bent to peer under the tablecloth, and when they bent I got a multiple whiff of mothballs. The mouth of each peering face was grinning broadly and showing unnaturally sharp teeth at the extremities. Hands on all four sides of the table reached for me and I shrank from them, but there was a limit to how small I could make myself. When the fingers of one of the males touched me, I struck them with my porridge spoon, but he knocked the spoon aside, dragged me from my poor hiding place, and sprawled me on the Axminster. Then all six were standing over me, grinning sharply. I was trapped, I was helpless. All I could do was stare up at their eager faces, quivering in terror as they bent over me, and—

'Hold!'

A stern voice from across the room. We all glanced towards a tall, thin gent in a grey frock coat, grey trousers, grey shoes, who stood in the open hearth. Everything about the newcomer was grey, even his eyes, his slicked-back hair, the moustache that stood out like pipe-cleaners, twirled at the ends. His greyness was spoiled only by a smattering of sooty smudges on his clothing.

'He iz miiine,' the grey man said in a rich foreign accent.

The six who bent over me straightened up, no longer grinning. 'We need nourishment,' one of the ladies said.

'Nourish yourselves elseverre,' the foreign gentleman answered, rolling every 'r' in sight. 'Zat vun iz spoken forr.'

The six looked disappointed, but they flapped their arms, turned back into bats, and flew up the chimney from whence they'd come.

Now it was just me and the grey man, who was so tall and imposing and serious that he made me as nervous as all the others put together. Still, I managed to get to my feet and ask him what was going on.

'Vot iz going on,' he replied, 'iz zat I have saved yourr miserable life.' He gave a small bow. 'Count Zornob.'

'Sorry?' I said.

His pale eyes glinted, as if daring me to mispronounce his name. 'Count Zorrrrrnob! And you arre...?'

I stuck my chest out and hoped I looked bolder than I felt. Hoped I sounded it too when I said: 'Jerome Ignatius Granville Offal-Trype.'

His grey eyebrows rose. 'Zat iz quvite a mouseful,' he said.

'I know. Call me Jiggy, it's easier. Now kindly tell me why you're here.'

He leant towards me. 'Do you not...recognise me?'

'No, should I?'

''Ve met yesterday, in *Ze Small Nocturnal Mammals House*.'

'There were a few people there when I arrived,' I said, 'but I didn't actually *meet* any of them.'

'I voz not vun of ze *people*,' he said.

With this he flapped his arms and, like the half dozen who'd just left, turned into a bat. A very pale one.

'*Now* do you know me?' said a voice in my head.

'The bat that peed on me!' I cried.

The pale bat fluttered its wings and turned back into the Count.

'I did not peee on you,' he answered – not in my head this time.

'You didn't? Oh, so it wasn't pee. Whew, that's a relief.'

'No. It voz speet.'

'Speet?'

'I spat at you.'

'Spat? You spat at me? That was *spit* I was covered in?'

'It voz.'

I was shocked. 'Why did you do that? What had I done to you?'

'I voz merely clearing my throat. I did not see you cowering zerre. I did apologise,' he added.

'Yes, you did – but I smelt so bad afterwards that no one would come near me till I'd had a bath, and I hate baths!'

The Count shrugged. 'Fresh bat speet does not please ze nostreels of Live Vuns, but vunce it iz vashed off zey can no longerr smell it. Zat iz good, iz it not?'

'Ha!' I said. This was not a laugh.

'Vot iz perhaps not so good iz zat ven bat speet lands on human skin it iz absorbed into ze bloodstream, verre it remains.'

'Remains?'

'Forr life. Until yourr dying day. And vampirres can smell it. Ve have very sensitive nostreels, you know.'

'V-vampires?' I stammered.

He went on as if I hadn't s-spoken. 'I should tell you zat any Live Vun whose blood contains vampirre speet iz a delicacy to uzzerrs of my kind,' he said. 'Zose six vould have drained you to ze last drop had I not come to yourr rescue.'

'Are you a v-vampire too then?'

He drew himself up to his full height. 'I am not just *any* vampirre!' he said proudly. 'I am of ancient arristrocracy! Vhy else do you sink zose commonerrs left vissout argument?'

'Is that why you're paler than other bats? Because you're an aristocrat?'

He brushed invisible crumbs off one of his lapels and tried to look modest. 'Zat iz so.'

'The bats in *The Small Nocturnal Mammals House* seemed pretty keen to stay out of your way too,' I said.

He snorted. 'Zem! Common-orr-garden bats! Not even vampirres in bat form. Zey vill not enterr *my* cave again, I sink!'

'Oh, you sleep there?'

'I do. I feel safe zerre from Live Vuns who vould slay me given half a chance.'

'Are there many vampires round here?' I asked mildly.

'Ve arre everyverre,' he replied.

'All draining people's blood?'

'Blood iz *all* zat ve consume.' But then he gave a wistful sigh. 'Sometimes I dream of eggs and bacon, ze odd mushroom, a tomato orr two, but my stomach turns ven I approach a plate of such sings. Vunce, a long time ago, I asked a stage hypnotist to help me overr zat, but...'

'But?'

'I voz peckish and sank my teeth into him and drank razzerr too deeply, turning him into vun of us.'

'What did he have to say about that?'

'He voz not grateful. He became my most forrmidable enemy. Ze Hypnovamp iz—'

'The Hypnovamp?'

'It iz vot he calls himself. Ven ze Hypnovamp turns his gaze on a Live Vun zat person iz helpless to resist.'

'The six who were here just now,' I said. 'There won't be any more like them, will there?'

'Any morre?' He put his hands on his hips, threw his head back, and laughed in a high-pitched, aristocratic sort of way. I glanced at the door, hoping Mother hadn't heard. 'Zey verr merely ze first,' the Count said. 'Viz my speet in your bloodstream every vampirre for miles around vill smell you and vant a piece of you. Zat iz vhy I have come – to varn you.'

'Warn me?'

'Zat if you vish to survive you must slay zem.'

'What do you mean...slay them?'

'I mean keell them.'

'Keell them? Me? What do I know about keelling vampires?'

'Morre zan you sink, perhaps,' he said. 'Did you not throw vun out of ze vindow last night?'

'He was a vampire?'

'No, he voz a vicarr who had filed his teeth to a point. Vot did you sink he voz?'

I chose to rise above the sarcasm. 'How'd you know about him anyway?'

'I felt a leettle responsible forr you afterr contaminating yourr blood, and—'

'I should think so too.'

'—and as you have my speet vizzin you I voz able to track you viz my bat senses. I voz flying by ven you threw him out.'

'I didn't throw him out. I just took a swipe at him and he lost his balance. He was too big to be chucked out of a window by me.'

'In zat,' said Count Zornob, 'you arre mistaken. Vampirre speet on human skin gives ze vearer certain…powerrs.'

'Powers?'

'Against my kind.'

'What sort of powers?'

'You vill find out ven zey attack you.'

'And you're sure they will attack me?'

'Oh yes. Zerre vill be no peace forr you from zis day forth.'

I sat down in front of my spoonless porridge bowl. 'This is not good,' I said, not meaning the porridge.

'If it helps,' said the Count, 'you could sink of yourself as ze Chosen Vun.'

I glared at him. 'Chosen One? I wasn't chosen, I was spat on.'

'Indeed you vere, but Chosen Vun has morre of a ring to it zan Spat Upon Vun, don't you feel?'

I shoved my jaw into my palms. 'What am I to *do*?' I wailed at the world at large.

'Vot you must do,' the Count replied on the world's behalf, 'iz keep a supply of my speet handy to dab on your skin in emergencies.'

'And that'll do the trick, will it?'

'Nine times out of ten, yes. Probably.'

'And the one time out of ten it doesn't?'

'You should run forr yourr life. Do you have a small containerr forr me to speet in?'

'No, sorry, containers for spitting in are in short supply in this house.'

'Ah, zat vill do.'

He plucked a small glass salt cellar from the sideboard.

'You can't use that,' I said. 'Father will notice it's full of spit when he tries to sprinkle salt on his food.'

'You must remove it,' the Count said. 'Blame its disappearance on a servant.'

'We haven't got a servant.'

He stared. 'Vot, not vun?'

I shook my head. 'We're trade. Well, Father is, which means Mother and I have to be too, like it or not.'

'I am sorry to hearr zat. It must be difficult forr

yourr poorr mozzerr, doing everysing herself.'

'Oh, she'd like you,' I said.

He unscrewed the top of the salt cellar and tipped the contents into the fireless grate. Then he spat several times into the pot before holding it up to the light.

'Zat should give you enough to fight a few battles.'

'I don't want to fight battles,' I said. 'All I want is to tuck my legs under me and read adventure stories by lamplight and have a normal life.'

He smiled a small tight smile. 'A fine ambition, but vun you must now fit in between murderous attacks frrom vampirres keen to drink yourr blood.'

'Jerome, have you finished your breakfast?'

Mother. Out in the hall.

'Almost!' I shouted. 'Father will be wanting me,' I whispered to the Count. 'I have to go on my rounds.'

'Rounds?'

'I deliver his meat. The meat he cuts for customers, I mean.'

'In zat case,' he said, 'I advise you to keep looking overr yourr shoulderr. Neverr assume zat

45

you arre safe from vampirrekind.'

'But I'm safe in broad daylight, surely? Vampires only come out at night, don't they – like bats?'

His lips twitched with amusement. 'Ve can valk abroad on grey orr misty days like today. As long as ze sun iz concealed, you arre in dangerr.' He handed me the pot of spit. 'You vould be vise to keep zis vizzin reach at all times.'

I pulled a face. 'I've got to sprinkle your spit on myself?'

'You could try, but ze holes arre too small for speet to get through. You must unscrew ze top, dip a fingerr in, and dab it on – behind ze earrs, perhaps, like cologne.'

I sniffed the pot.

'It stinks.'

'It vill cease to stink ven it touches yourr skin. Uzzerr Live Vuns vill still smell it, but not you.'

I put the former salt cellar in my dressing gown pocket. I did not thank him.

'The vampire who went out of my window yesterday,' I said. 'When he fell on the railings below, he—'

'Jerome! Come *along*!'

Mother again, and her voice was nearer.

'I must go, I sink, viz some haste,' said the Count.

He stepped into the hearth, flapped his arms, became a grey bat once again, and flew up the chimney a second before Mother stormed in and ordered me to get dressed. I pushed past her.

I was not in a good mood.

CHAPTER FOUR

Mother was again on the step when I was dressed
and went downstairs, but she wasn't sweeping this
time. I caught a flash of green as someone she'd
been talking to left her. She came inside and closed
the door rather too quickly. 'About time,' she said.
'Get on now or there'll be complaints.'

'Complaints?'

'About late deliveries.'

'Why are your cheeks all red?' I asked.

Her eyes slid sideways. 'It's chilly out there. Go.'

I took a breath and opened the door off the
hall. As usual when I went through to the
shop I clenched my nostrils and averted my eyes
from the dangling carcasses and trays of offal on
the counter. There were no customers, just
Father sawing through the ribs of some poor dead
animal.

'Late this morning, Jig,' he said.

'Sorry. The lumps in Mother's porridge jammed up my throat.'

'You really should try black pudding, y'know.'

'I did. I was throwing up for days.'

He sighed. I was a lost cause. 'I've wrapped the orders,' he said sadly. 'You'd better get off.'

I didn't need telling twice, because as much as I hate delivering his little parcels of meat, at least I'm out in the fresh air. Well, the foggy air. As I've said, it was a very grey November. I put my hat and apron on, arranged the addressed packages in the basket, and pushed my bicycle into the alley alongside the shop.

There were three new customers on today's list, but even if there'd been no unfamiliar addresses to find, this morning would have been like no other. Vampires keen to drain my blood? Now that was worrying. Because of this possibility I had put the former salt cellar in my pocket so that I might dab myself with its contents at short notice. I did not see how a drop of spit could save me from the kind of teeth I'd seen of late, but I had no other means of defence. The threat of attack made me suspicious of every approaching stranger, and I glanced about constantly for fear a particularly toothsome person might sneak up on me or leap out of the fog. But nothing of the sort happened, and after a while I relaxed and just got on with the job. I rang bell after bell, rapped knocker after knocker, handed over package after package to whoever answered, giving the respectful little salute Father insisted upon if it was a householder who answered rather than a mere servant.

The fog remained thick all morning, but it wasn't so dense that I could not find my way to the new addresses. I saved the last of these – one of the cottages near the railway embankment – to the very end, as a sort of reward. I love trains: the sight of them, their speed, their smell. As I approached the cottages I heard the sound I'd hoped to hear and, leaning the bicycle against the fence that fronted the cottage gardens, I ran to the rise and looked along the line. A passenger train was rushing out of the tunnel of fog that clung to the tracks. Half-deafened by the sound, happily blinded by the engine's gushing smoke as it lumbered below me, I imagined being in charge of one of those mighty beasts; pulling the levers, shovelling the coal into the furnace, and whatever else you have to do to keep it going. 'Wonder how you get to be an engine driver?' I mused as the train and its carriages rattled into the distance.

'I expect you have to write to the railway company,' said a voice behind me.

I jumped. I hadn't realised I'd spoken out loud, or that I wasn't alone. Turning, I smelt mothballs. The man who stood behind me wore a faded check suit, a scuffed bowler hat, and was very pale, with a sharp nose.

'Is that your cottage by any chance, sir?' I asked, indicating the address I was to deliver to.

'Oh, I don't live near *here*,' he answered, and before my eyes his lips extended to reveal at their widest stretch a pair of long, pointed teeth.

My throat went dry. 'You're not a vam...vam...'

'I'm guessing that "pire" is the syllable you're searching for,' he said.

I glanced behind me. I was no more than a yard from the edge of the embankment. Should I jump over? It was a long way down to the tracks, and I might twist my ankle when I landed. If that happened I wouldn't be able to run and the vampire would no doubt pounce on me and do his worst. I recalled a similar difficulty that a MacIntyre-Quiver character had once found himself in. A couple of ruffians were hard on the hero's heels, firing pistols at him as he fled. Bullets whistled past his ear. One parted his hair. But then he came to the end of a dark alley, knew he couldn't escape, and pretended to have been hit and killed. Thinking he was dead, the villains walked away chortling, and the hero lived to fight another day. But that was just a story. If I pretended to have been killed by a leap to the railway tracks, my blood would still be warm. Warm blood would be fine with the vampire, who would waste no time in sucking it out of my body. I doubted I'd be able to get up and walk away after that.

I was thinking these things when the vamp gripped my shoulders, sending my hat flying.

'Can we discuss this?' I asked hopefully.

He eyed my neck hungrily. 'Let's not,' he said.

I reached surreptitiously into my pocket. 'Please, think of my poor mother. I'm her only child. She'll miss me.'

'Am I expected to care?' he replied.

'Well, I'm new to vampires,' I said, unscrewing the spit pot with one hand, 'but I wouldn't be surprised to learn that you're very caring people deep down.'

He sniggered. 'Being so new to us, you might also not be surprised to learn that you couldn't be more wrong.'

As he drew his head back and prepared to plunge those dreadful points into my neck, I tipped a small dollop of the former salt cellar's contents into my palm and gave the lid a half screw to secure it. I smelt the vamp spit briefly, but once it touched my skin I smelt nothing. I don't know what I expected to happen next – I certainly felt no more powerful – but just as my attacker's mouth came down, my fist shot up to meet it, rather firmly. He staggered back.

'What have you done?' he gasped, staring at the broken points of his two sharpest teeth on the ground.

In reply, I brought my hatless head up under his jaw. I felt nothing, but he crumpled, and down he went. I reached for him, but before I could get a grip on his lapel he was up and off, holding his mouth.

'You! Boy! What's going on?'

A large hand gripped my shoulder from behind. Oh no, I thought, another one. I spun round, and, with a cry of 'Take that!', punched him in the stomach.*

'Oof!' gasped my new assailant; but he recovered quickly and lifted me off the ground by my armpits. I swung my fists and kicked his shins, but though he cried out he did not release me or reel as the first vampire had done. I was just wondering if the power of the spit on my skin had worn off already when I noticed that, unlike the others, he wasn't showing sharp side teeth but gritting very ordinary ones.

'Officer!' he shouted to someone behind me. 'Quick!'

Next thing I knew another man had gripped my arm. I carried on struggling, but between them the two held me fast.

'Keep this up, son,' said the second man, 'and you'll feel my stick across your…eeeaargh, what is that *stink*?!'

---

* Q's heroes hardly ever hit anyone without saying 'Take that!' or something like it.

As he and the first man's noses jerked in the air to rise above the odour of vamp spit, I realised that he was a policeman and stopped struggling.

'Sorry,' I said. 'I thought you two were vampi—'

'Silence!' The policeman held me out at arm's length. 'Heavens, boy, you need a wash. What happened?' he asked the other man.

'I live over there,' the man replied, 'and I heard a commotion and came to my window and saw him beating up a gentleman.'

'Where's the gent?'

'He ran for it, and who can blame him, set upon by a young thug.'

'I'm not a thug,' I said, 'and it wasn't the way it looked.'

'Save it for the magistrate,' the officer said. 'Come along, my lad!'

With that, holding his nose, he hauled me off to the police station.

CHAPTER FIVE

I wasn't charged with anything at the station because once the desk sergeant got a whiff of me he thought of some more urgent business and just put me in a cell to 'cool off'. It was a very dismal cell: rough brick walls, bars over the little window – too high to see out of – the only furniture a hard, narrow bed, which I sat on the edge of thinking how unfair this was. All I wanted was a quiet life reading about the adventures of made-up characters, and here I was thrown into the clink after an adventure of my own, a real one, which I'd neither wanted nor sought, and certainly hadn't enjoyed. I was sighing over all this when I heard a fluttering at the window. I glanced up, expecting to see a bird there.

It wasn't a bird.

It was a bat.

I jumped to my feet and reached for the spit pot, which I had not declared when ordered to turn out my pockets by the sergeant.

'Relax, it iz I,' said a voice in my head, and the bat flapped and took the tall, grey, moustachioed form of Count Zornob.

'What do you want?' I demanded, leaving the spit pot in my pocket.

'Zat iz a fine velcome,' he said haughtily.

'Yes, well, I'm not exactly thrilled to be in here.'

He looked about him. 'It iz as good a place as any to continue ourr chat. Less chance of interruptions, perhaps.'

'Till my parents get here,' I said miserably.

'Oh, zey know you arre herre?'

'An officer's been sent to tell them.'

He smiled. 'I imagine you arre not looking forward to *zat* interview.'

'No. Mother will give me hell.'

He waved my dread away. 'Zat iz what mozzerr's arre forr. You and I must make ze most of zis interlude to talk morre of yourr new life as a vampirre slayerr.'

'Vampire slayer?' I said. 'New life?' I said. 'No,' I said. 'Listen,' I said. 'I don't want to make a *career* of it.'

'Oh, so you sink you have a choice, do you?'

'Well, there must be some way I can get out of it.'

'Zerre iz. You allow one of my kind to keell you.'

'You don't seem all that bothered about your lot being beaten,' I said.

He glanced at his fingernails, which I noticed for the first time were longer than normal. 'Vampirres arre not known for zeirr loyalty.'

'In that case, how do I know *I* can trust you?'

'You do not. But if I might continue?'

I sank back onto the side of the bed. 'All right, go on.'

He positioned himself before me, hands clasped behind his back. 'Let us begin viz *yourr* quvestions. I imagine you have some?'

'I have one,' I said.

'Only vun? You surprise me. But ask it.'

'Why can I only hear your voice in my head when you're a bat?'

He sighed. 'Not a very bright quvestion if I may say so.'

'Why?'

'Bats cannot speak. Surely you knew zat.'

'Oh. Yes. All right, mothballs.'

'Mothballs?'

'Yes. You don't smell of them, but all the others do.'

'Zat iz because ze uzzers sleep in vardrobes,' the Count said.

'Wardrobes? You're joking.'

'No. I used to myself, until I moved to my leettle cave.'

'I thought vampires slept in coffins.'

He chuckled. 'A myth. One of several invented by writerrs of melodramas.'

'How do you sleep in a wardrobe?'

He shrugged. 'You go in, you close ze doorrs, zen yourr eyes, and…sleep.'

'What, standing up?'

'Yes. Ze trouble viz vardrobes, howeverr, iz zat moths arre drawn to zem, and zey neebble at us vhile ve—'

'Neebble? Oh, nibble.'

'—vhile ve slumberr, so ve stick mothballs in ourr pockets to repel zem. I do not use zem in my cave because moths do not bozzerr me zerre.'

'Any other vampire myths I should know about?' I enquired.

'Vun orr two, perhaps. Crosses and silverr, forr instance. According to yourr legends, ve arre afraid of crosses, but a cross iz no morre harmful to us zan a circle orr squvare. Ve do get a leetle bit quveasy ven ve see an equvilateral triangle, but zat iz anozzerr story.'

'And silver?'

'Silverr, yes. You might have heard zat ve can be keelled by silverr bullets.' He shook his head. 'Silverr goes right through us. It does us no morre harm zan vooden stakes.'

'I thought a stake through the heart finished a vampire off,' I said.

He grinned. 'A vampirre's internal organs arre no longerr living, zo vhy should a piece of vood harm zem? Overr ze centuries many Live Vuns have come afterr us armed viz stakes, to ourr very great amusement. No, zerre arre only two sings zat can keell us.'

I leant forward expectantly. 'And they are?'

'If I tell you,' he replied, 'you must promise to keep it to yourself.'

'You have my word.'

'Very vell zen. Iron and graphite.'

'Graphite? As in the lead of a pencil?'

'Yes. Insert ze tiniest sing made of iron or graphite into any part of us and ve arre vell and truly knackered. If zat got out, humans vould hunt us down viz iron bicycle spokes orr pencils and ve vould soon become an endangered species.'

'Oh,' I said. 'So when the vamp who fell out of my window landed on the railings, the *iron* railings...'

'He vos turned instantly to screaming dust. Had ze railings been made of some uzzer material – apart frrom graphite, of course – he vould have picked himself off zem and strolled away in search of a bloody nightcap.'

'How about decapitation?'

'Decapitation?'

'I mean if a vamp's head was cut off, would it...slow him down a bit?'

The Count squirmed and felt his neck. 'It vould. Please, I beg you, do not spread zat around eizzerr. But talking of necks...' His gaze had fallen on my own neck and he licked his lips. 'I missed my elevenses.'

I pulled my collar up around my ears. 'Keep your

peepers off. I don't want to be turned into a vampire.'

'Only if morre zan a pint iz taken by an individual vampirre can a Live Vun be turned,' he said, 'but you have nussing to fear. My speet in yourr bloodstream vould prevent yourr being turrned by anyvun – especially me. I am sorry, no eternal death forr *you*, my young friend!'

'There is one other thing I'd like explained,' I said. 'Since the visit to the zoo everything smells stronger. The meat in Father's shop, Mother's perfume (which was bad enough before), the horse manure in the street, even the fog.'

'My speet in yourr bloodstream also heightens yourr sense of smell,' the Count said. 'You vill get used to—'

'Quiet!' I hissed.

'Vot?' he said.

'Listen!'

He listened. So did I. Footsteps on flagstones, the jangle of keys.

'Interruptions, interruptions,' the Count said irritably. 'Again ve must postpone ourr chat!'

He flapped his arms, became a bat once more,

and flew between the high bars in the nick of time.

'Your pater's here, lad,' a deep voice said: the policeman who'd gone to tell my parents I'd been arrested. Father was right behind him.

'What've you been up to, Jig?' he asked as the officer unlocked the cell door.

'It's all a horrible misunderstanding,' I said.

The copper laughed, not in a nice way. 'Well, that's a new one.'

Fifteen minutes later I was released into my father's charge – after he paid a fine and I was given a serious warning about assaulting innocent people. 'Right,' he said as we left the station. 'Now let's hear your side.'

I dared not tell him the complete truth. I knew that if I started going on about vampires he would cuff my ear for talking nonsense. So I simplified my story.

'I was about to make a delivery to the new customer near the railway embankment when a man came at me out of the fog. I thought he was going to attack me and lashed out. It was the fog. Made me jumpy.'

'Is that what you told the police?' he asked.

'More or less. They didn't believe me. Do you?'

He stopped walking and put a hand on my shoulder. 'If you say it's so, son, it's good enough for me.'

'Thanks,' I said. I was quite touched.

'But I suggest we keep this whole incident from your mother.'

'She doesn't know already?'

'No. She was out when the bluebottle called.'

'Whew.'

'Yes…'

There was something about the way he said 'Yes…'.

'Something wrong?' I asked.

'No.'

But there was, I could tell. 'Come on, what is it?'

He gave in. 'I think your mother might be sweet on someone.'

'Sweet on someone?'

'Another bloke.'

I was shocked. 'What makes you think that?'

'Well, you know the way she gets when some chap says nice things to her? Goes all soppy and coy, and blushes to her hairline.'

'Mm...'

'She was like that when she went out earlier, but worse than usual, like someone's been paying her *special* compliments.'

I remembered the person Mother had been talking to on the step earlier. Was that who Father was suspicious of?

We were almost back at the shop when he realised that I didn't have my bicycle.

'It got left behind at the embankment when I was arrested,' I told him. He hadn't noticed that my hat was also missing and I had no plans to point it out.

'You better go and fetch it,' he said. 'And I just hope for your sake that it hasn't been nicked — the meat on it either.'

'There was only one more delivery on it,' I said.

'That's one delivery I can't afford to replace, especially after paying hefty fines at cop shops. Run along now, and get back here sharpish.'

I ran along. And this time I kept my eyes well peeled for grinning people with sharper than normal side teeth.

CHAPTER SIX

As I didn't have to follow a delivery route this time, I took a short cut through the Rantingdown shopping arcade. I was about halfway along it when I saw my mother looking in one of the shop windows ahead of me. And she wasn't alone. I flung myself into the recessed doorway of a tobacconist's, but Mother's head turned a second too soon. I stayed put anyway, hoping she'd think I hadn't noticed her, but luck wasn't on my side today. I smelt that eye-watering perfume of hers before I heard her.

'Jerome! What are you doing here?'

I turned, all innocent. 'Oh, hello, Mother. I was just wondering how soon I could start smoking a pipe.'

'A pipe?'

I waved a hand at the window full of smoking paraphernalia and tobacco advertisements. 'I like that one.' I pointed to a briar with the face of a little devil standing out in relief on the bowl.

'Jerome, you are not to start that filthy habit until you turn sixteen,' Mother said. 'If you must smoke then, your father will buy you a pipe.'

'Oh, all right,' I said. 'I was only looking anyway…'

I trailed off because her companion had joined us, and he was someone you couldn't ignore up close. He was a thick-set man in a suit of deep burgundy, a fancy green waistcoat with a pocket watch on a chain, and a cape that matched the waistcoat. Small round spectacles were balanced on the end of a podgy little nose, he had a short, perfectly trimmed black beard, and he wore a top hat. Such an appearance would have made him stand out in any crowd, but it wasn't the look of him that made me struggle for breath, it was his scent, which was even more nostril-shrivelling than Mother's, but so sweet, like a sultan-sized box of *Hazer Baba Turkish Delight*.

'This is Mr Mallaki,' Mother said. She had to introduce him, but she was clearly embarrassed about being seen with him. 'And this is Jerome,' she said to her friend.

'Delighted to make your acquaintance, Jerome,' the gentleman said, touching the rim of his hat and gazing at me over his little specs in a curious sort of way.

'Well, we must be off,' Mother said, and, with what seemed to me undue haste, she took the man's arm and walked him away. I watched them go, unhappily. Father was right. Mother had a fancy man. A *very* fancy man.

I was thinking about this all the way to the embankment. Worrying about it. What would happen now? Would Mother leave us? Would it be just Father and me and the meat? Without Mother to make the porridge I might *have* to eat bits of carcass at breakfast. So preoccupied was I with these unpleasant possibilities that I barely looked up until I neared my destination. My bicycle was where I'd left it, against the fence. I looked in the basket. The last parcel was gone.

'You,' a voice said. 'Back again.'

The speaker was walking up the path of the nearest cottage. It was the man who had summoned the police officer and had me arrested.

'This is my delivery bicycle,' I explained.

'Yes, I realised it must be after you'd been taken away.'

I pointed to my apron. 'Never seen a butcher's apron before?'

'I might have noticed it if you hadn't set about me.'

'I thought you were going to attack me,' I said.

'I don't go round attacking kids,' said he. 'Let you off then, did they?'

'My father paid a fine.'

'Ah. Well, I took out my liver.'

'I beg your pardon?'

He tapped the side of my basket. 'The package with my address on?'

I looked at the number on his gate. Seven.

'Oh, it was yours. I was going to deliver it when...' I stopped. No point going over all that again. 'All right if I take my bicycle?'

'Go ahead, I don't want it.' He went back indoors.

I fished in my pocket for my little delivery pad, slid the thin pencil out of the spine, and crossed out his address. If he ordered more meat from our shop, Father could deliver it. Putting my pad away, I noticed my hat lying upturned on the ground. I picked it up, dusted it off, put it on.

I did not get on my bicycle immediately, but steered it away from the cottages. I was some way along the track when a little old lady in a shawl emerged so suddenly from the fog just ahead of me that I had to swerve to avoid her.

'Morning, young man,' she said in a creaky voice.

'That's your opinion,' I muttered, and carried on, head down. I'd done enough chatting to strangers for one day.

'Nice day for it,' she said as I passed her.

'Hm!' I said.

But then I thought: nice day? It was a terrible day. Even if everything had gone really well since breakfast it was grey, damp and still foggy. I glanced at the woman. You see ancients like her all the time, shuffling along, mumbling to themselves or talking to the first person they meet. She smiled when our eyes met, and when she smiled I smelt mothballs. I froze, but then remembered that old people and mothballs go together, like tea and milk, toast and marmalade, pigs and swill, and smirked at the fear that had shivered through me. I was about to go on my way when I noticed something at the corners of the old lady's widening smile. She leant towards me.

'You smell good,' she murmured, placing a bony hand on each of my shoulders.

'It's all the baths,' I answered, thinking that maybe when you're so old that you smell of mothballs your side teeth go all pointy and long, like hers.

I would have stepped out of her ancient grasp, but her fingers tightened. Quite a grip for an oldie, I thought as the hand on my left shoulder twitched aside my collar. It was only when her head went back and her biddyish old mouth opened wide that I came to my senses – this wasn't just *any* old lady! – and jumped back, broke her grip, and shoved my bicycle between her and me.

'Now just a minute, madam,' I said.

'Oh, it'll take longer than a *minute*,' she answered. 'I'm going to make the most of a delicacy like *you*, young fellow!'

With this she leapt over the bicycle as though

her heels were on springs and came down flat-footed on my side of it. I gulped. Unless I acted quickly I would be done for. I felt in my pocket for the spit pot.

'Do stand still, there's a good boy,' the old vampire lady said, once again grabbing my shoulders.

'Sorry,' I said. 'I get sort of jittery when I meet vampires.'

'Never mind, you'll be quite still in a minute. What's that you have there?'

I'd been having trouble unscrewing the ex salt cellar with one hand and had taken it out.

'Oh, it's nothing, it's just – oops!'

I said 'oops!' because I'd dropped the spit pot. Fortunately the glass didn't break when it hit the ground, but with the old vampire's surprisingly strong hands holding my shoulders I couldn't stoop to retrieve it. The only other thing I had left to defend myself with was my little notebook. Hardly a weapon, I thought, but in desperation I took it out, thinking that a slap across the trap might slow her down for a sec. I wasn't quick enough. Her teeth came down so swiftly that my only recourse was to jerk sideways, but in the jerking I dropped the notebook too, which left me holding nothing but the little pencil that had been slotted into the spine. The sideways jerk caused my attacker's teeth to sink into my collar rather than my neck, which did not seem to improve her mood.

'Stand *still*, wretch!' she said fiercely.

I glanced about, hoping that someone was racing to my rescue. Silly idea. Even if the fog hadn't been too dense to see any distance, if someone came upon us they would almost certainly think that it was I who was attacking the old lady rather than the other way round. Knowing that another minute would see me lying on the ground, bloodless, pale, dead, all I could hope to do was delay the end as long as possible by protesting and trying to ward her off. I was doing this quite vigorously when an agonised scream filled my ears and a wrinkled balloon of vamp dust swirled to the ground on which the old woman had stood. Was it something I said?

Or did?

I looked at my hands. All that either of them held was my little notebook's pencil, whose lead had snapped in the tussle. Some of Count Zornob's words came back to me:

'Insert ze tiniest sing made of iron or graphite into any part of us and ve arre vell and truly knackered.'

So that was it. In my flailing terror the point of my pencil had pierced the old vamp's skin. Interesting. When your enemy was a vampire, a pencil was even mightier than a sword!

CHAPTER SEVEN

It was a Wednesday, half-day closing, the one day I didn't have to help in the shop after my round. Good news usually, but that particular Wednesday was my first target-for-vampires day, which rather took the edge off my pleasure.

I decided to spend the afternoon indoors.

There were fireplaces in most of the rooms in our flat, but for economy's sake Mother only lit fires in a couple of them, which meant that vampires might come down any of the other chimneys in their bat forms. However, if their senses drew them to me alone, it seemed likely that they would come to wherever I was, and I didn't like the idea of that, so I went to my bedroom, where there was no fireplace at all.

It was chilly in my room, but huddling inside a blanket in my armchair I was soon lost in chapter eleven of Q's latest, *Danger in the Dunes*. It was an exciting part. The hero, Major A.R.M. Pitt, pursued on horseback by a gang of unshaven sand pirates, had dug himself a hole amid the dunes. The Major (Pongo to his pals) had covered himself with sand and was breathing through a straw he always carried for such purposes. His enemies, waving scimitars and baying for blood, were keen to catch and torture him for thwarting their plans to steal an Arab prince's jewels. They were so close now that a hoof of one of their horses might plunge into his hole at any moment and—

'Eeek!'

I didn't say this because the sand pirates had discovered the Major, but because I was once again made unexpectedly aware of bats – seven or eight of them, pressed against my foggy window, gnashing their sharp little teeth at me. My MacIntyre-Quiver flew into the air as I jumped out of the chair, dropped my blanket, and raced to my bedside table. I snatched the former salt cellar, unscrewed it, dabbed the Count's spit on my neck, and turned to face them – just as Mother came in.

'Jerome, I wanted a word with you about...' She stopped. 'What are you doing?'

What I was doing was standing beside the bed with my hands balled into fists, all set to fight the bats if they broke the glass.

'I'm…acting,' I said.

'Acting?'

'I'm reading Q's new novel, and Pongo's besieged by—'

'Pongo?'

'The hero. These sand pirates are trying to get him, you see, and I got sort of caught up in the action, and…'

I dried up because she'd stopped listening. I can always tell when my mother's no longer with me from the drift of her eyes. Another reason for not going on was that the bats had retreated into the mist. Maybe it was the sight of Mother. I often feel like retreating into mist at the sight of her myself.

'Jerome,' she said, sniffing sharply, 'what's that…?'

'What's what?'

She came closer, sniffed some more, and recoiled as though I'd smacked her across the nose with a dead rat. 'It's the same smell as yesterday, at the zoological gardens!'

It was the freshly dabbed vamp spit, of course. As before, I couldn't smell it myself because it was on my skin. But she could. Oh yes, she could!

'Are they the same clothes?' Mother asked, hankying her nose.

'Same clothes as what?'

'That you were wearing yesterday.'

I was wearing the same underpants, but I didn't intend to tell her that because (a) it was private, and (b) she'd be furious.

'Same shirt,' I said. It wasn't, but I had to give her something.

'Well, take it off this instant.' She backed towards the door. 'Then put it in the bath to soak – after you've done the same.'

'The same?'

'Soaked yourself *thoroughly*.'

'In the bath?'

'Of course in the bath.'

'Mother, I had my second bath in a week just yesterday.'

'So you did, and you'll have another now.'

'I can't,' I said. 'The extra one was bad enough, but a third could finish me. Didn't you see that article?'

'What article?'

'In last week's paper. The Medical Practitioners' Society says that if a male person bathes more than twice in one week his skin softens and he starts buying flowers and fluffing up cushions.'

'Oh, you do talk nonsense, Jerome. You'll take another bath or be confined to this room for a week.'

'If I'm confined to my room,' I countered, 'I won't be able to deliver Father's meat and help in the shop. All right, it's a deal.'

'Your confinement will begin *after* you've done your day's work.'

So much for that then. In spite of the vampire problem I couldn't stay in my room for a whole week because I was over halfway through my book and would need to get another from the library in a day or two.

'All right!' I said. 'I'll take yet *another* bath!'

'And I'll see you into it,' she said.

'No you won't,' I said.

'Oh, but I will,' she said.

'Mother,' I said, 'I'm a growing boy. I do not need an elderly female parent putting me in the bath. In fact, I won't allow it.'

She crocheted her eyebrows together and glared at me. 'You're not too big to fit over my knee, Jerome Offal-Trype.'

'I think I am,' I said.

Her eyebrows parted company. She knew I was right. I was already as tall as her. If she put me over her knee both ends of me would trail on the carpet, and my weight would probably crush her legs.

'What did you come in for anyway?' I asked as she turned away.

'It'll keep. Later, when you've got rid of that…eergh!'

She shuddered and flounced out.

I went to the bathroom, locked the door, and ran the bath as ordered. But I didn't get into it, I just slushed the water noisily around a bit and scrubbed the vamp spit off my neck with a bar of coal tar. The rest of the time I sat on the floor reading *Danger in the Dunes*.

After my 'bath' Mother sniffed me. 'Acceptable,' she said.

'More than you are,' I muttered.

She cocked her head suspiciously. 'Meaning?'

'That farmyard scent you douse yourself in. It shouldn't be legal.'

She tossed her nose in the air (though it remained stuck to her face). 'For your information, some people find my perfume rather appealing.'

'Some people?' I said. 'Your *friend*, for instance?'

'Friend?'

'From the arcade. Mr Malarkey.'

'Mr *Mallaki*,' she said, in a way that Q would describe as 'tartly'.

'That's the one.'

'Now that you remind me, it was he whom I wished to speak to you about earlier.'

'I don't want to hear it,' I said sourly.

'I simply wanted to inform you that he's a gentleman I met by chance who just happens to share my taste for...elegance.'

'Oh, another snob then.'

'I'm not a snob, Jerome, and neither is Mr Mallaki. He's a man of learning and refinement. I don't meet many such as he these days.'

'Since you married a butcher, you mean.'

'Jerome, please, I don't mean that at all.'

But I knew that she did. 'And this Mr Mallaki,

he likes that killer scent of yours, does he?' I asked.

'As a matter of fact, he does, yes.'

'And I bet you like his.' This seemed to puzzle her. 'Don't say you haven't noticed how sickly sweet he smells,' I said.

'I've noticed no such thing,' she snapped, but I could tell by the way her eyes slid to the carpet that she *had* noticed, and wasn't revolted by it. Poor Father. He didn't stand a chance against a 'refined' gentleman who stank of something his wife found more appealing than dead meat.

Unfortunately, my first meeting with Mother's gentleman friend wasn't to be my last. The following morning, riding home after completing my round, I heard a voice behind me.

'I say. Jerome, isn't it?'

I stopped my bicycle and turned in the saddle. There he was.

'Ye-es…' I made out that I couldn't place him, though it would have been hard not to as he still wore the burgundy suit and green cape and waistcoat and smelt as nauseatingly sweet as before.

He peered at me over his little spectacles, smiling ever so slightly. 'We met yesterday. Rantingdown Arcade. I was with your mother.'

'Oh, yes,' I said, as if it had just come back to me.

I saw his nostrils twitch, like he was sniffing me – *he*, smelling like that, sniffing *me*! – and a small frown rumpled the bit of brow that could be seen beneath the rim of his hat. Eager as I was to put distance between us, I held his gaze as a point of honour, as one of Q's heroes would have done.

'Charming lady, your mother,' Mr Mallaki said.

'I'm sure she'd be flattered to hear your opinion,' I answered.

'She's heard it already.'

He looked even more intently into my eyes as he said this, as though keen to make sure that I understood his meaning.

I blinked and glanced away.

'Another foggy day,' I said lamely.

'But a fine one for a tryst in the park,' he answered.

I looked back at him. 'A what?'

'I have someone to meet there.'

'Oh, right. Well, enjoy yourself.'

I pedalled away in haste, wondering why Mother would be drawn to such a toad.

At home, I deposited the bicycle in the alley, went into the cold-room behind the shop, and hung up my hat. Through the half-open connecting door, I could see Father slicing ham. I don't remember thinking anything at all as I turned to one of the carcasses hanging from a row of meat hooks and sank my teeth into it. Sank them, tore at the flesh, and chewed. The uncooked meat required quite a bit of tooth work, but I kept at it until—

'Jig, what are you doing?'

I stopped chewing. Father stood in the doorway. 'Mm?' I said.

And all in an instant the foul taste of raw pig struck my taste buds and my mouth fell open. Half-chewed meat fell out.

Father grinned. 'Trying to get a taste for it to please me, eh? Well, much as I appreciate the effort, son, you should know that meat isn't generally eaten off the hook.' The shop bell clanged. 'But now that you've turned the corner,' he said, 'I'll have to ask your mother to make us one of

Granny Offal's delicious mixed meat casseroles.'

He went through to attend to his customer.

My father might not have been so pleased with me if he'd seen me rush out into the alley and vomit behind the dustbins. I was still there, on my knees, when a voice spoke.

'Feeling poorrly, my friend?'

I got to my feet dragging an arm across my mouth.

'I've just done something dreadful,' I said to Count Zornob. 'I...'

As the thought of it filled my mind I doubled over and vomited again.

'I sensed zat somesing voz amiss viz you,' the Count said, 'and cut my yoga lesson short. It iz probably just as well. My yoga teacherr's neck iz just too tempting forr such as I.'

I had other things to think about than yoga teachers' necks.

'Do you know what I just did?' I said, raising my head. 'I ate raw pig. And I even hate *cooked* meat!'

'If you dislike it so much, vot made you eat it?'

'I don't know, I wasn't thinking, I just...' I shrugged helplessly.

He rolled one end of his moustache between a finger and thumb. 'Did you, perchance,' he said thoughtfully, 'have company recently?'

I spat aside. I could still taste that poor dead pig. 'Company?'

'A conversation viz somevun you do not know vell, perhaps?'

'No. Well, only my mother's fancy man.'

'Fancy man?'

'I bumped into him in the street. I don't care for him.'

'Vot does he look like?'

'Look like? Well, he's…he's…'

I'm not much good at describing people, and besides, I didn't want to even *think* about that gentleman.

'Do you know verre he vent afterr you parted?' the Count asked.

'The park, I think. He said something about meeting someone there.'

'Zen I sink ve too should go to ze park. I vould like to see zis fancy man viz mine own eyes.'

'Go ahead,' I said. 'I've seen all I want to of him.'

He pulled himself up to his full grey height

and frowned down at me.

'You must accompany me. How vill I know him if you arre not viz me?'

'That's true,' I said. 'But—'

'But nussing,' the Count said firmly. 'Come!'

I sighed. Took my apron off. My life just wasn't my own any more.

'Very well. But if we see him, don't ask me to speak to him, all right?'

CHAPTER EIGHT

On the way to the park, the Count said: 'I do not like ze look of zis fog. I sink ze sun iz trying to break through.'

Now that he mentioned it, the fog was definitely brighter than it had been. 'What if it manages it?' I asked.

'Zen I make myself scarce, very, very quvickly.'

'And if you're too slow?'

'My skin peels.'

Although the fog was brightening it was still too dense to see more than eight or ten yards in any direction. It also muffled sound, so perhaps it's not surprising that as we walked the main thoroughfare through the park we failed to hear the carriage that plunged suddenly out of the mist. We jumped aside only just in time.

'Watch where you're going, you blithering idiot!' the Count shouted at the driver.

'Blithering idiot yourself!' the man retorted, whipping his horse. 'Keep off the road!'

I looked at the Count in surprise. His angry shout hadn't contained a trace of accent. I was still wondering about this when he flung an arm across my chest.

'Oof!' I said.

'Quiet!' he hissed.

'I was until you hit me in the chest,' I said. 'What's up?'

'I sense heem.' His accent was back. Maybe anger makes you lose your accent if you're foreign, I thought.

'Sense who?'

'Heem. My old enemy.'

'Which old enemy? You must have quite a—'

He clamped a hand over my mouth. Only when I'd assured him with my eyes that I would keep it shut did he release me.

'Ve must step varily,' he whispered. 'Forvard now, but vith carre.'

'Wait a minute,' I said. 'If he's one of yours and you can sense him, can't he sense you too?'

'Maybe not, if his senses arre…distracted.'

'Distracted?'

'Enough of ze quvestions. Come along!'

And together, with him in front, we worked our way silently forward, from one tree trunk to the next along the side of the road. When the Count stopped at last, forcing me to stop too, I saw, in the thinning fog, a man and woman seated on a bench. At about the same time two familiar scents, intermingled, flared my newly sensitive nostrils.

'Mother!' I cried, for one of the scents was hers.

'Oh, vell done,' groaned the Count. It wasn't a congratulation.

Not surprisingly, Mother had heard me. 'Jerome?' she said, turning.

She saw me peering round the tree, but not the Count, who'd flipped sideways so as to conceal himself from her and her friend.

'Do not mention me,' he muttered, pushing me out into the open.

'What are you doing here?' Mother asked, rising.

'I could ask you the same thing,' I said.

'I was…taking a stroll,' she answered, obviously embarrassed to be caught out like this.

'We meet again, Jerome.'

Her friend had also risen. It was Mr Mallaki. So it was my mother he'd been on his way to meet!

'Voteverr you do, do not look into his eyes,' the Count whispered.

I glanced at him, puzzled. What *could* he mean?

But Mr Mallaki noticed my trunkward glance. 'Is there someone there with you?' he said.

Realising that the game was up, the Count also stepped out.

'There is,' said he.

The change that came over Mr Mallaki at the sight of him was startling. His eyes popped, his fingers sprang out like twigs, and his lip curled. 'You!' he snarled.

'Me!' the Count confirmed. 'This meeting is long overdue, Mallaki.'

Once again he'd spoken without the accent.

'Overdue indeed,' Mother's friend replied, eyes glinting over his little spectacles. 'Well, Wobblebottom, and how is this going to work?'

I felt my eyebrows lift. Wobblebottom? Not the finest insult I'd ever heard, but, well, it was short notice.

'You two know each other?' I asked the Count.

'Oh, we know each other,' he answered, still without the accent.

'Mr Mallaki,' Mother said to her chum, 'what's going on here?'

He did not answer, or even seem very much aware of her now. Mother and I stared at him and the Count as they squared up to one another.

'You're not going to fight, are you?' I said. 'Come on, grown men...well, one grown man and one vam—' I glanced at Mother. 'Two grown men scrapping in a park. Not very civilised.'

I'm sure they would indeed have fought if, just then, a shaft of brilliant sunshine had not illuminated the path between them, whereupon they yelped like a pair of kicked puppies, and fled in opposite directions.

And what did I do? Stay with Mother? Follow the Count? No, I took off after Mr Mallaki. I wasn't sure why, only that I felt compelled to see where he went. As he scuttled away his top hat flew off. He did not stop to retrieve it, but ran on, arms folded over his exposed head.

Now that the sun had pierced the fog, the mist

quickly dissolved, which helped me keep track of Mr M where I would have had difficulty doing so minutes earlier. As he reached the road that encircled the park the sun burst gloriously through the last of the fog, and he sank to his knees as though brought down by it. But then he flung his arms out, waggled them frantically, and…

…turned into a bat.

As a bat he flew shakily towards the large apartment block across the road and, reaching the third storey, flew through a small open window and was lost from sight.

That evening, hearing a fluttering at my window, I reached for the spit pot, ready to dab some of its contents on myself if more of my enemies had turned up. But drawing back the curtains, I saw only one bat: a grey one. I opened the window just enough for it to fly in. It flapped its wings and turned into Count Zornob, who now wore a thick cloak – grey, naturally.

'I hoped I'd seen the last of you and your lot,' I muttered, closing the window.

'No such luck,' said he. 'You're stuck with us for

life, however long or short that turns out to be.'

'What happened to the accent?'

He shrugged. 'There doesn't seem much point in keeping it up now that you've heard my real one.'

'I did wonder about it,' I said. 'It was the craziest accent I ever heard.'

'It's a very *fine* accent.' He sounded offended. 'Honed to perfection over decades.'

'Why do you use it?'

'Because, traditionally, vampire counts have rich mid-European accents. A foreign aristovamp is still looked up to by the lower orders of my kind.'

'I'm guessing you're not a real count then.'

'No. But don't tell any of the others.'

'I wasn't planning on having coffee mornings with them. Who are you really?'

'Well, my birth name was Maurice Wobble-bottom…'

I smirked. 'So it wasn't an insult, it's your name.'

'My *original* name. One joke about it and I'll drain you of your last drop of blood in spite of my New Year's resolution to watch the calories.'

'It's nowhere near New Year,' I said. 'The last one anyway.'

'A vampire's New Year starts the day he or she was turned. My turning occurred on the 24th of October, seventy-three years ago.'

'And you changed your name right away?'

'No, I was undead for a full decade before I did that. It had become clear to me in that time that Maurice Wobblebottom wasn't a tremendously appropriate handle for a merciless bloodsucker.'

'Good point. But if you're not really a count why are you so pale when you turn into a bat?'

'I had an albino grandfather. I seem to have inherited some of his genes.'

'And who's Mr Mallaki?'

'Remember the stage hypnotist I told you that I turned once upon a time? The immortal enemy who calls himself the Hypnovamp?'

'That's him?'

'Yes. It's because of what he can do with his eyes that I warned you not to look into them. If he fixes a Live One with his hypnotic gaze he can make him or her do anything – as he's already proved to you.'

'Me? He hasn't made me do anything.'

'Oh, so you took a mouthful of raw pig for

the experience, did you?'

'Oh!' I slapped my forehead. 'When I met him on his way to the park!'

The not-really-a-count Count nodded. 'Until I found you throwing up after eating raw meat I had no idea he was even *in* this part of the world.'

'You think he's tracked you down?'

'I doubt it. Coincidence, I expect. He seemed genuinely shocked to see me.'

'But why would he make me eat raw meat?'

'Who knows? Maybe he took a dislike to you. I can see how he might.'

'But he's befriended my mother…'

'It'll be her perfume. Mallaki always did have a weakness for strong scents. Look at the one he wears – powerful, *and* it covers the smell of mothballs. I wonder where he keeps his wardrobe?'

'Why do you care?'

'The time has come,' the Count replied, 'for one of us to cease to be undead. To become, simply, dead.'

'I have a fair idea where his wardrobe is,' I said.

'You do? How?'

'When the two of you ran off I followed him to

an apartment building. I even saw which window he went in.'

'He climbed in?'

'Flew in. As a bat.'

'Ah,' said the Count. (I couldn't think of him as Mr Wobblebottom.) 'You must take me there. Right away.'

'Take you there? To a vampire's wardrobe? At night?' I shook my head. 'I think not.'

'But you have to. Only you know where it is.'

'I'll draw you a map.'

At this he came over all nervous. 'To tell you the truth, I'd be glad of the company. He's a powerful fellow.'

'A powerful *vampire*. I'm just a boy.'

'A boy,' he said, 'who, with my spit on his skin, has the power to slay my kind, or at least fight them off in small numbers. You could be quite an asset to me against the Hypnovamp.'

'It's not my fight.'

'I'll be eternally grateful.'

'That's because you'll live forever. I won't.'

'Please?' he said, suddenly quite pathetic.

'Oh…'

After sneaking out to the landing for my winter coat, I climbed down the drainpipe. The Count flew down as a bat. In the street, he regained his human form and we set off together for the second time that day. I wasn't at all happy about this. I liked my dangerous adventures in stories, not real life. My life anyway.

CHAPTER NINE

On reaching our destination, I pointed to the window Mr Mallaki had gone in by.

'We have to get into that apartment,' the Count said grimly.

'Easy for you,' I said, 'not for me.'

He shook his head. 'You don't need wings to get up there.'

'Why? Got a very tall folding ladder tucked inside your cloak?'

'Have you never heard of lifts?' he said, charging across the road without looking to see if anything was coming. I looked for both of us, hoping to delay events by having to wait for a carriage or omnibus to pass. The street was deserted. I crossed the road, dreading what might happen inside that building.

The Count pushed open the double doors and held one of them for me. A man at a highly polished desk glanced up from a newspaper. He was about to speak, probably ask if he could help us, but the Count got in first. 'Good eevening,' he said, in that overripe phoney accent of his, and flounced by in a swirl of cloak. He seemed so at home there that the man must have taken him for an owner or tenant he hadn't met before, so he returned a 'Good evening, sir,' and let us go. I kept my head down as I followed the Count across the lobby.

The lift was already on the ground floor, so we didn't have to wait for it. We stepped inside and the Count pulled the mesh door across and pressed the number three button. As the cage began its ascent, he said, as Maurice Wobblebottom, 'The way to get on in your world is to act like you own it. I learnt that way back. A show of confidence can get you past all manner of awkward questions.'

'Doesn't work with my mother,' I muttered.

When the lift stopped at the third floor, the Count yanked the door back and we stepped out. There were doors at intervals all along the carpeted corridor, both to the left and the right of us.

'Which way?'

I'd rather lost my bearings since entering the building and the lift.

'The window you indicated looks out over the park, which is that way,' the Count said, setting off without hesitation. 'The sixth window in from the western elevation.'

I was impressed. That was the sort of detail a Q hero would notice. As we approached the door we sought, however, the Count faltered. Not looking forward to what we might have to do, I was trailing behind him, but when he came to an abrupt halt I had no choice but to join him.

'What now?' I asked.

'We break in.'

'Break in? Couldn't we just knock?'

'Knock? Oh, what a good idea. And when he opens the door? "Hello, might we come in and turn you to dust, old chap?", is that it?'

'We can't be sure he's at home,' I said. 'I mean, vampires sleep in the daytime and go out at night, don't they?'

'As a rule, yes, but when the sun hides, as it's been doing so often of late, many of us go out during the day and catch up on the beauty sleep later. I myself batnapped at the cave earlier.' He gripped me by the shoulders and looked me very seriously in the eyes. 'Good luck,' he said.

'Good luck? With what?'

'With what? What do you think? You're the vampire slayer.'

I shook him off. 'You expect me to go in there and challenge a powerful hypnotist-type vampire on my own? That's not what you said back at the shop. You asked me to accompany you, that's all.'

'If I'd said that you would be leading the charge, not me, you might not have come,' he said.

'Might not?' I said. '*Might* not? I absolutely wouldn't have!'

'Well, you're here now, so face up to it. Go on.'

'No.'

'But you must, it's your job.'

'My job?' I said. 'Correction. My job is reluctant meat delivery boy.'

'That was before you were spat upon by a vampire bat.'

'By you.'

He waved a hand at the technicality. 'The point is, you're now a liquid diet for all vampires unless you get them first. Do stop arguing. Dab yourself with the spit I put in that salt cellar and get to it.'

'If he's so powerful, how do you know it'll work against him?' I asked.

'If it doesn't, I'll wipe away a tear and compose a sickeningly sentimental note of commiseration to your parents.'

'That's a comfort.' I felt in my pocket for the spit pot. Then I felt in another. And the rest. 'Um…'

'What?' he said.

'I seem to have left it at home.'

'*You left the essential vampire spit at home?*' he gasped in incredulous italics.

'Mm.'

'*The vampire spit that will give you the power to defeat our enemy?*' he added, in the same kind of italics.

'Yes. In my other coat. Ah well.'

I turned to go. He grabbed my shoulder from behind.

'Fortunately,' he said, 'I'm here.'

'How is that fortunate?' I asked, turning.

'I'll give you some more of my spit.'

'But I don't have another bottle.'

'No need.'

He cleared his throat and spat on my forehead. Warm vamp spit ran between my eyes and started down my nose. I would have wiped it away, but a hand shot out and gripped my sleeve.

'Don't!' he said. 'It won't work if you wipe it off!' I lowered my arm – reluctantly. 'Now, lad, prepare to fight the Hypnovamp.'

'We have to get in there first,' I reminded him.

'No problem for a vampire. Stand aside. Watch and learn!'

I stood aside, I watched, I learnt, as he gathered himself together, charged the door, struck it with his shoulder, and bounced off.

'Impressive,' I said.

'Out of practice!' he snapped, rubbing his shoulder.

He gathered himself together a second time and once again ran at the door shoulder-first. He might even have managed to break through this time if the door hadn't opened an instant before he reached it. But such was his momentum that he could not stop, and he charged into the room beyond, across it, and—

CRASH!

—through the window.

'Aaaaaaaarrrrggggg!'

His yell got smaller and smaller until its place was taken by a tiny, pavement-type thud.

While the little lady who had opened the door stared at the large Count-sized hole in her window, I sniffed her. No mothballs. She turned to me, and although she looked a little puzzled, said, 'Visitors, how nice. I was just making myself a nice cup of tea. Do join me.'

A nice cup of tea sounded just the ticket on such a chilly night.

'Thanks,' I said.

I stepped inside. She closed the door.

'Make yourself comfy,' she said. 'Won't be a mo.'

She trotted to the kitchen and I seated myself on the sofa and gazed around the pleasant flat. I felt kind of relieved actually. This was so much better than calling on a bloodsucking vampire.

In a minute the lady returned with a tray of tea things, which included a plate of fairy cakes. As she set the tray down she frowned at me.

'Oh dear, what's that on your face?'

'My face? Oh, it's…'

I could hardly say 'vampire spit', so I left the explanation unfinished.

She wrinkled her nose. 'It doesn't smell very nice, whatever it is. Here, let me.' She took out a little lace hanky and dabbed my face thoroughly. 'There. Much better. Now. The tea!'

It was Earl Grey with lemon, the way my mother takes it. I usually have it with milk, but the home-made fairy cakes made up for that.

'Sorry about the window,' I said, while we were sipping and nibbling.

'It's a cold night with that hole,' she said.

I got up and drew the curtains. 'Better?'

'Oh yes, thank you.' I sat down again. 'Your friend,' she said then, 'did he…want something?'

'We're doing a survey on the strength of window glass,' I said.

'Oh, I see.' She giggled. 'The things that are done these days! Have another cake, dear.'

I was about to reach for one when there was a knock.

'I'll get it,' I said.

I got up and went to the door. The Count stood

without, dishevelled and damp, the twizzles on the ends of his moustache drooping and dripping.

'Has it started to rain?' I asked.

He ignored this. 'I worked it out,' he said.

'Worked what out?'

'We were looking at the third set of windows up from the pavement, but we came to the third floor in the lift, forgetting that the first floor is the one above the ground floor, which means that the third set of windows belongs to the second floor the lift goes to. We came one floor too far.'

'You're sure about that?'

'Absolutely, even though I just fell several floors onto my head.' He peered over my shoulder at the lady. 'Apologies for the window, madam. Please send me the bill.'

'How kind,' she answered sweetly. 'I'll need an address.'

'43, Doggerel Mansions, West One. Good evening to you.' He pulled me out of the flat and strode along the corridor with his arm round my shoulders to make sure I went with him.

'43, Doggerel Mansions?' I asked.

'Never heard of it, but I could hardly say The Bat

Cave, Zoological Gardens, could I?'

We took the stairs to the next floor down and approached the door we should have gone to the first time.

'Are you going to pull the same stunt as before?' I asked the Count.

'You mean go crashing through the window?'

'I mean charge at the door.'

'No. This time I'll use a key.'

'A key? You have a key?'

From deep within his cloak he took a strange-looking implement with prongs that quivered in all directions.

'Can't think why it slipped my mind last time. Maybe because I don't often have cause to use it.'

'Funny-looking key.'

'It's a vampire key. Fits any lock, but only if a vamp inserts it. In your hands it wouldn't fit anything on earth.'

When he touched the lock with the prongs of the strange key they felt their way inside. They must have made it a perfect fit, for when the Count turned it the door opened with a spine-tingling creak. His lips twitched.

'Vampire sound effects, don't you just love 'em?' He became serious again. 'Now. We must locate his wardrobe.'

'A bedroom seems the best bet for that,' I said.

'Not necessarily. As we don't use beds there's no guarantee there is one. It could be in the kitchen. Not that we have much use for kitchens either, other than to store bottles of blood for wet nights when we don't fancy going out in search of fresh. After you, lad!'

CHAPTER TEN

The room we entered contained a large couch, a couple of comfortable-looking armchairs, a sideboard, and a dining table and chairs. There were paintings of horses on the walls.

'It doesn't look very vampirish,' I said dubiously.

'What do you want,' the Count replied, 'blood running down the wallpaper, cobwebs hanging from the ceiling, skeletons in the chairs? Trust me, this is where he comes to sleep.'

'I trusted you last time.'

'Never trust a vampire's first promise,' he said.

'And his second?'

'He rarely makes a second.' He opened a door off the sitting room, turned and mouthed the word 'kitchen' at me. Then he mouthed: 'Look for the bedroom.'

'You said it might not be in the bedroom,' I mouthed back.

'What?' he mouthed.

I went to him and, seeing as he couldn't read lips, whispered, 'You said the wardrobe might not be in the bedroom.'

'No,' he whispered back, 'but as he's probably renting this – or has killed the owner – it seems likely that there was one there when he moved in.'

He opened a couple more doors. The first was the bathroom's, the second belonged to a broom cupboard – no space for a wardrobe in either. Just one door remained. The Count opened it with particular care, as if expecting his enemy to leap out wielding an axe or something. No one leapt out. He nodded at me. I joined him at the door. An ordinary bedroom lay beyond, with an ordinary double bed, a jug and basin on a marble-topped dresser, a loaded bookcase, and...a big double wardrobe. I felt my Adam's apple bob.

'I suppose it might just be *clothes* in there,' I whispered optimistically.

'No,' the Count whispered back. 'I sense him. He's in there all right.'

'And you're sure he's asleep?'

He tiptoed to the wardrobe, listened at one of

the closed doors, tiptoed back. 'I hear him snoring. Get ready.'

'What's the procedure?' I asked.

'Procedure? There isn't one. We make it up as we go along. I thought we might fling the doors back and stick him with that iron bar.'

'What iron bar?'

'The one inside your coat.'

'I haven't got an iron bar inside my coat.'

'All right, the thing made of graphite.'

'I haven't got a thing made of graphite either.'

He stared, then gripped my elbow and steered it out of the room along with the rest of me. He pulled the door to behind us.

'You didn't bring anything made of iron *or* graphite?'

'I didn't know I was supposed to.'

'But I told you that graphite and iron are the only things that can kill us apart from lopping our heads off.'

'Pity you didn't remind me of that before we started out,' I said with fake sorrow. 'Oh well, better call it a night as we have nothing to kill him with.'

'After all the trouble we had finding him?' said the Count. 'No, we're here, he's dozing, it's our big chance. You'll have to do it by hand, that's all.'

'By hand?'

'Boy to vamp combat. You stand a small chance of coming out of it with your heart and kidneys in the same place they are now.' He inspected my face. 'My spit appears to have sunk in already. Well, no matter. Even absorbed, the power of fresh vamp spit lasts an hour or so.'

I would have told him about the little old lady wiping it off, but he was already back in the bedroom. I sighed and followed, wishing I was curled up at home with my MacIntyre-Quiver.

Gripping the twin handles of the wardrobe doors, the Count glanced over his shoulder, mouthed 'Ready?', and, before I could mouth 'No', flung the doors wide and jumped aside, affording me a grandstand view of its contents. The only clothes inside were a paisley silk dressing gown, a burgundy suit, a green cape and waistcoat, and a set of frilly shirts. The rest of the space was taken up by Mr Mallaki, standing to attention in fancy red satin pyjamas, eyes shut, arms crossed over his chest, smelling as sickly sweet as ever. He no longer wore his specs and his hair was perfect. He looked so peaceful standing there, and normal, if a man standing in a wardrobe with his eyes shut can ever look normal.

The Count gestured silently for me to approach. I gestured just as silently for him to accompany me to the bedroom door. He looked a trifle exasperated as he did so.

'What? Cold feet?'

'Cold feet and every other part. I want to go home.'

'Oh, do you?' he said. 'Well, feel free.'

This sounded like good news. 'You mean I can?' I said hopefully.

'Certainly. As soon as you've despatched the Hypnovamp.'

The hope withered on the vine. 'How about tomorrow? Tomorrow always seems such a good day for things like vampire killing.'

'You're not very bold, are you?' he said.

'No.' I wasn't ashamed to admit it. I was a simple butcher's son, not a simple action man.

'Wouldn't you like to do something heroic for once in your life?' he asked.

'I'd rather read about other people doing it,' I confessed.

'Imagine when you're old,' he said.

'What for?'

'You're looking back over your life, thinking of all the things you've done, and there's absolutely nothing that stands out as being special.'

'And I suppose,' I said, 'that that's meant to make me think, "By Jove, he's right, I must do something really brave right away, such as kill his archenemy, the vampire with the hypnotic eyes". Well, it doesn't. Goodnight.'

I turned away.

'Oh, don't go.'

I stopped. The reason I stopped wasn't because the Count had said, 'Oh, don't go', but because someone else had. I turned back. Slowly. The Count also turned, just as slowly, and together we stared at the bedroom door, in which Mr Mallaki stood in his gorgeous satin pyjamas.

'I do so *love* guests,' he said, flashing pointy side teeth at me. 'Especially young ones. So tasty.'

'Over to you, Jiggy,' said the Count, putting me in front of him.

It was the first time he'd called me by my name, but I didn't spend a lot of time thinking 'How nice'. No, the thought I was having was 'How the hell do I get out of this?'

'You keep the wrong company, my young friend,' said Mr M.

'I'm not the only one,' I said.

'If you mean your mother, I meant what I said about her being a charming woman. I look forward to draining her blood and turning her into my undead companion.'

'You leave my mother alone.' There was a limit. I could just about put up with her as she was, but the prospect of her as a vampire, still bossing me about when I was old, was too much.

Mr Mallaki laughed and looked over my shoulder. 'I'm guessing this isn't a social call, Wobblebottom.'

'You're right,' said the Count from behind me.

'And the boy's part in this is…?'

'Can't you smell him?'

Mr Mallaki's gaze returned to me. He frowned,

and leant closer. I recoiled. That scent of his!

'There's something there,' he said, sniffing me.

'If you didn't wear such odorous cologne,' the Count said, 'you might have detected it earlier.'

'You don't mean…?'

'Yes. He carries my spit in his bloodstream.'

Mr Mallaki gazed at me with fresh interest and licked his lips. 'In that case, I could have a very pleasant midnight snack.'

'You could,' said the Count, 'if it wasn't also on his skin.'

Mr Mallaki took a sharp step back. 'His skin?'

'Yes. Get him, Jiggy!'

I didn't get him, of course. I couldn't have. But the Count didn't know that, and neither did Mr Mallaki, who must have decided that now would be a splendid time to make his departure, for he shoved me aside, kicked the Count in the stomach, waggled his elbows, turned into a bat, and crashed through the window. Vampires seemed to be rather fond of dramatic departures through unopened windows.

'Why didn't you stop him?' the Count wheezed, holding his stomach.

'I wouldn't have been able to,' I said.

'But you have the Power!'

'Er...not exactly.'

'What do you mean, not exactly?'

'You know the old lady on the floor above? While you were out she...' I hardly liked to say it.

'She what?'

'Wiped the spit off my face.'

'She *what*?'

'Wiped the spit off my face.'

'She wiped the spit off your face?'

'Yes.'

'And you *let* her?'

'I didn't want to hurt her feelings, especially as you'd just turned her window into a door.'

'You might have mentioned this before,' the Count said.

'I would have, but everything was happening so fast.'

'Hm! Well, we can't let him get away now he knows we're after him. Present your face! I must spit on it again!'

I offered him the palm of my left hand. 'This is all you're getting.'

'Oh, it's not *nearly* as theatrical,' he said, but spat in my palm. He folded my hand – 'Take *care* of it this time!' – flapped his elbows, and turned into his bat self. 'Follow me!' he said in my head, veering towards the window.

'You mean I have the power to jump out of windows and not go crashing to the ground like you did earlier?' I asked.

He paused. 'Good thing you mentioned that. Take the lift. Meet me outside. Hurry now, no time to lose!'

CHAPTER ELEVEN

When I walked across the lobby from the lift, the man at the desk looked up from his paper. 'All right, son?' I said that I was, but his brow creased as I passed. 'What's that smell?'

I folded the hand that contained the vamp spit. 'What smell?'

I pulled my collar up and stepped out into the rain.

'Took your time, didn't you?' a voice said in my head.

'Had to wait for the lift, it was on another floor. Where are you?'

A flapping sound from above me. The albino bat was hanging upside down in the building's porch.

'Well do try and keep up, there's a good chap. Off we go.'

'Which way?'

'Just follow me. I'm tracking him with my

incredibly sharp bat senses.'

He took off along the perimeter of the park and I crossed the street and went after him, keeping my left hand lightly closed so the rain wouldn't wash the spit off. We were the only boy and bat about, though the occasional gentleman and couple hurried by holding hats or umbrellas. There was very little traffic.

Soon, still in the wake of the bat-Count, I was running towards the railway embankment, which I hadn't planned to return to for a while after the events of the day before. As the thunder growled and the lightning shivered, I heard, in my head, the words, 'He's stopped. I think he's waiting for us.'

Splashing to a halt in a puddle I peered through the slanting rain. A shaft of lightning briefly illuminated the Hypnobat suspended by his feet from one of the trees overhanging the tracks.

'Now what?' I asked when the bat-Count flew back to me.

'Now you sort him out.'

'He's up a tree. I can't fly, remember?'

'Yes. Pity about that. We'll have to get him down to your level.'

'How do we do that?'

'You taunt him.'

'Taunt him?'

'Insult him, call him names, say anything to antagonise him. And when he rushes at you in a fury, you spring into action. Don't worry, you won't be able to help yoursel—'

He was cut short by a crash of lightning so close that we both jumped. The lightning did not illuminate the bat in the tree this time, however. There was a reason for this.

'Where'd he go?' the Count wondered.

'Behiiiiiiiind you,' said a singsong voice straight out of pantomime.

We turned. Mr Mallaki, no longer a bat, stood there in his red satin pyjamas. Rather wet ones.

'Do your stuff, Jiggy,' the Count said in my head.

'Stay where you are, boy!' cried Mr Mallaki. 'I'll deal with you when your friend's a little heap of dust at my feet.'

Before either of us could react, he grabbed the albino bat and pinned its wings to its sides, preventing it from flapping them and returning to the Count's human form.

'I think,' said the Hypnovamp to the bat in his hand, 'that I shall bite your head off. A quicker end than you deserve, Wobblebottom, but it's such a miserable night, and satin is *so* uncomfortable when wet.'

So saying, he opened his mouth and drew the helpless creature slowly towards him, clearly intent on milking the big revenge scene.

'Jiggy... Jiggy...'

This was the bat-Count. Its eyes, very round and frightened, were begging me to save it. I almost resisted the plea – I owed the Count nothing, after all – but I hesitated too long, and during that hesitation I realised that I couldn't allow his head to be bitten off. I reached out to stay Mr Mallaki's arm and to my surprise he cried out in pain, his hand flew open, and he dropped his intended victim. While he massaged his arm, the albino bat flapped its wings and turned into the Count, tall and proud in his swirling grey cloak.

'You see?' he said. 'With my spit on you, you don't know your own strength.'

'You'll pay for that,' Mallaki growled at me. 'And don't think you can defeat me. It'll take more than a drop of Wobblebottom's spit to see *me* off. Once I've disposed of him I'll drain you of every last drop and throw you in the gutter to be trampled by horses and torn apart by dogs.'

'You're not a very nice man, are you?' I said.

'Man?' he said. 'I'm not a man at *all*, thanks to your friend here!'

With this, he threw himself upon the Count, and then the two of them were rolling around in the pelting rain, gnashing their teeth, trying to gouge eyes out and tear ears off, using knees, fingers, feet, and all manner of ungentlemanly manoeuvres in pursuit of victory. Then, as if by mutual agreement, the tussling two turned themselves into bats and flew upward. At first, the Hypnobat was the pursuer, but then the Count's bat turned on him, and they began whirling round and round one another, spitting and baring teeth as sharp as tiny knives. Between the tangled branches of the trees they spun and spat, and all I could do was watch, wonder how this would turn out, and wish I was safely tucked up at home with *Danger in the Dunes*.

'Who wants first dibs?' a voice behind me said.

I turned. A lady and three gentlemen stood

there. The lady and one of the gents carried umbrellas. They looked ordinary enough, were dressed in ordinary clothes and all, but even in the rain I could smell mothballs.

'May I help you?' I asked.

'Indeed you may,' one of the men replied. 'Bare your neck, there's a good fellow.'

'Why would I do that?' I said, playing for time.

'Oh please,' the lady vampire said. 'I hate the rain. Let's just get it over with, shall we?'

I might have argued for a while in hope of delaying what looked like being my sorry fate if not for a distracting shout from above. All five of us looked up. The Count and Mr Mallaki had reverted to their human forms but were still fighting, balanced precariously on the broad bough of an old oak.

'Instead of going for me,' I said, turning to my new acquaintances, 'why not give the Count a hand?'

'The Count?' one of the vampire gents enquired.

'The one in grey. The other's the Hypnovamp. He's not nice.'

'Of course he's not nice, he's a vampire.'

'Yes, but he's *especially* bad. Here's your chance to show your good side. Do something decent for a change.'

The four glanced at one another as if they were really considering this. Then they burst out laughing.

'Decent side! The boy's living in a fantasy world. Get him!'

Two umbrellas were tossed aside and all four vampires flashed their sharpest teeth before stepping forward as one, while I, also as one, stepped back. One of the males reached for me. His nails were at least three inches long, and sharp as daggers. Nails like those could rip the flesh from human bones without any trouble, I thought. What chance did I have against such nails, to say nothing of all those teeth? I raised my hands, hoping the four would take pity on my youth and troop back to their wardrobes. A forlorn hope, of course, but as the long-nailed fingers were about to close on my wrists, one of my hands folded into a fist and struck their owner's nose, which crunched like a set of small dry twigs. He reeled and the others hesitated, but then one of them said,

'Lucky punch,' and also reached for me. He too did not manage to grab me, however, for my other hand shot out and knuckled his ear, hard, which caused him to fall sideways and knock the lady vamp off-balance.

And then it was all action – my action – as my fists, elbows, feet and knees flew at my opponents without the slightest instruction from my brain. My opponents seemed rather taken aback by this flurry of activity, as well they might. Drawn to the bat spit in my bloodstream, they could not have known of the fresher spit in my palm, and the power it gave me to resist them. Once they overcame their shock the four spread out and came at me from different directions, but my body, if not my mind, was ready for such a ruse. I jumped in the air and whirled like a demented dervish, kicking and lashing out, and few of my blows failed to connect with some part of one or more of them.

I did well enough without weapons of any kind, but somewhere in all this furious kerfuffle I found that I did after all have a pencil about me – only a stub, but its point was not entirely blunt and with it I stabbed the female and one of the males, who screamed themselves to dust which was washed away by the rain. Unfortunately, the second stab snapped the last of the small point, leaving me apparently defenceless. The surviving two, faces contorted with fury, were preparing to spring at me when there was a piercing screech from the trees. The Count and the Hypnovamp had once again turned into bats and were going at one another more feverishly than ever. Taking advantage of the distraction, I jerked a knee into the crotch of the nearest vampire and, when he folded, introduced my other knee to his chin while stabbing at his companion's eyes with two extended fingers. When the second vamp fell back, groping blindly, I leapt into the air and came down on his shoulders to squeeze his neck with all the strength in my thighs – a strength they'd never had before. I expected his pal to tear me from him, but he'd had enough. He fled, limping more than a bit. He might have done better to take his chances with me as it turned out, for as he hobbled away a tremendous lightning bolt shivered out of the drenched heavens and struck him between the shoulder blades like a silver spear. He screamed horribly and turned to dust that instantly mingled with the rain. I made a mental addition to my list of things that could kill vampires. Decapitation, iron, graphite, and now lightning.

'Enough! I surrender!'

This was the vampire whose shoulders I rode. But, unconvinced that he was giving in, I jumped off him and rabbit-punched his chest until he flapped his arms, turned into a bat, and flew off into the storm-riven night. Watching him go, thrilled to have discovered that I could defeat more than one vampire at a time, I felt like an Edric MacIntyre-Quiver hero, and it was good.

Before I could pat myself on the back too many times, however, an overhead shriek reminded me that the bat-formed Count and the Hypnovamp were still battling away. The Count was in retreat again, fluttering wings that seemed too weary to return him to his human form. I had to help him. But how? Whatever powers I possessed, flight was not among them, and there was little point in climbing up into the branches, for the two enemies were hopping from tree to tree. Was there nothing

I could do? No way that I could help the Count? In between these muddled thoughts and the ever louder roars of the thunder I heard a train steaming along the tracks below, but for once I did not rush to watch its approach with a smile on my face.

'Ah!'

I snatched up a stone that fitted neatly into my palm yet had a fair weight to it. Estimating where the Hypnobat would be seconds after the stone left my hand, I drew my arm back and hurled. It might not hurt him much, I thought, but there was a chance it would throw him off-balance and give the Count time to escape. My guess as to where my target would be shortly after the throw proved accurate enough, but I hadn't counted on the bat-Count rallying and rushing his foe, so that the stone did not knock just one of them clear of the trees, but both. I gasped in dismay as the dazed bats tumbled towards the tracks just in advance of the speeding train. Had I killed two bats with one stone?

Then a pair of things happened at one and the same time. As the vampire bats fell to the tracks a shaft of lightning struck a rail, in response to which the brakes of the rushing train squealed shrilly, though it travelled on for some way before grinding to a halt. It was a miracle that the engine and carriages did not leave the rails and that no lives were lost. No human lives anyway. I stared in horror as a solitary bat flew unsteadily up into the streaming thunderclouds. There was no lightning just then, so it was impossible to tell which it was – my friend, or the one who had vowed to despatch me without mercy.

CHAPTER TWELVE

I tried to sneak in, but Mother caught me. 'Jerome, where have you been? I've been worried sick.'

'I…'

'Well?'

'I…'

Hard questions to answer.

'And look at you,' she went on. 'Drenched from head to toe. I cannot *believe* that you went out on a night like this without an umbrella. You could have caught your death.'

'Some did,' I muttered.

'What was that?'

'I said you're so right. Foolish of me, I should know better.'

'You should. You're to have a hot bath immediately!'

'A bath?' I said. 'Mother, I'm wet. The last thing I want is to get wetter.'

'You'll do as I say,' she said, 'and you will not argue, do you hear?'

'I have no choice, you're shouting in my face, but Mother, I—'

'I *said*, Jerome, that you will not *argue*.'

'Yes. I know. But listen. That'll be four baths in a row. Four! Three's the absolute limit if you don't want my skin to go all saggy like yours.'

'My skin is not saggy,' she said, but glanced in the mirror to check, and tidied her hair while she was at it. Then she pointed out of the room.

'Go! And don't think you'll get away with sitting on the side of the bath *pretending* to be soaking in it.'

I tried not to gape at this. How did she know I did that? Was there a tiny hole in one of the bathroom walls through which she watched me reading when I should be bathing? In the bathroom, while running the water, I inspected the walls for secret spy holes. I found none, so maybe Mother was merely psychic. It wasn't the first time that that thought had crossed my mind. But I took the bath and was warmer for it, so it hadn't been such a bad idea after all.

I went to bed almost immediately afterwards, but as I curled up under the bedspread with *Danger in the Dunes*, my mind wandered from the daring deeds of Pongo Pitt. In the past twenty-four hours I, like him, had had perilous encounters and risked my life fighting formidable enemies. Who would have thought that I, Jerome Ignatius Granville Offal-Trype, the butcher's son who hated the sight and stink of blood, would become a fighting machine able to see off gangs of bloodthirsty vampires? I was lying there thinking back over all that had happened, my book on my chest, smile on my face, when I heard a rapping at the window that froze my blood. I tugged the blankets up to my chin and stared in terror at the closed curtains.

Rap-rap-rap!

There it was again.

Rap-rap-rap-rap!

And again.

'Who…who's there?'

Rap-rap-rap-rap-rap-RAP!

Whoever or whatever was the other side of the curtains probably hadn't heard my timid query, which left me with three choices.

1. To repeat it more loudly and risk my parents rushing in.
2. To pull the blankets over my head and hope my visitor would lose interest and go away.
3. To leap heroically out of bed and see who or what was out there.

All a'twitch and twither, my eye caught the cover of my novel. It showed the intrepid Major Pitt, square-jawed, steely-eyed, clench-fisted, confronting three leering, unshaven enemies with rifles. Would the great Pongo have hidden under the bedclothes when his enemies knocked at his window? I thought. Hadn't I proved that I was made of the same stuff as he? I thought next. And, I thought finally, if I had defeated my foes three times already (counting the old lady vamp in the shawl) surely I could do it again — couldn't I? I reached for my little pot of spit, only to remember that it was still in the jacket hanging on the rack in the hall.

Rap-rap-rap-rap-rap-rap-RAP-RAP-RAP!!!

The rapper or rappers seemed to be increasingly agitated. I visualised a great cloud of bats hovering out there, eager to transform themselves into their human shapes and take turns at my neck until I was blood-free. They were just the other side of the glass, which was breakable, and I had nothing to fight them with. No vampire spit, no decapitation device, no iron bar, not even a pencil.

But then...

'What is the *matter* with you? Why won't you let me in?'

These words did not meet my ears but were received inside my head, and the voice that framed them was familiar enough to catapult me from bed to window, where I twitched aside a curtain, cautiously in case I was in error. But I was not. Count Zornob was alive! As alive as any undead creature had a right to be anyway.

'Deaf, are you?' he said, hovering at the window in his bat form. 'Open up, it's wet out here.'

I raised the window and he sprayed me liberally as he flew in and parked himself on the back of my chair.

'I thought you were a goner back at the embankment,' I said, closing the window.

'You weren't the only one.'

'And the Hypnovamp?'

'He was underneath when we fell, so that he alone made contact with the railway line. While the iron of the track temporarily paralysed him I was thrown clear, and after the lightning struck the rail and the train went over him there wasn't an awful lot left of him.'

'You checked on that, did you?'

'Oh yes, I went back to make sure. His bat self was not only scorched furless but squashed pleasingly flat.'

'No chance of his coming back in his vamp form, I suppose?'

'None. If the bat gets it, so does the vampire, and vice versa.' The bat-Count shivered. 'I'm cold. Why don't you have a fire?'

'No chimney,' I said. 'Assume your human shape and I'll lend you my dressing gown. Bit small for you, but it should take the chill off.'

He shook his bat head sorrowfully. 'Even though I wasn't physically injured in the fall, I seem to be no longer quite myself.'

'How do you mean?'

He flapped his wings. Nothing happened.

'You're stuck like that?' I said.

'It appears so.'

'Ah. No more vampiring for you then, eh?'

'Other than as a bat, no. Can I stay with you?'

'Stay with me?'

'Yes.'

'Here?'

'Yes. I'll be no trouble. You could sneak blood up from your father's shop for me.'

'I thought vampires had to have human blood.'

'No, no. Human blood's tastiest, but when there's a shortage anything will do as long as it's not congealed. Can I? Stay? Here?'

'What's wrong with your cave at the zoo?'

'I don't want to go back there. My confidence seems to have taken a bit of a dive. I feel a need for the company of a kindred spirit.'

'I'm not your kindred spirit.'

'You're the nearest I've got, so you'll have to do. Look, you don't have to worry about my being seen. I can hide under the bed when someone comes in. And there would be an advantage to having me near.'

'Oh yes?'

He drew his batty grey head back and a little gob of spit smacked onto my cheek. 'You'll need a constant supply of that to keep your enemies at bay, and with me here you'll never run out.'

'Comforting as that sounds,' I said, 'there are no enemies here just now, so if you don't mind…'

I stooped and wiped my cheek on the bed-cover.

'They might not be here *now*,' he replied, 'but cross my bat heart and hope to live, when they hear about you or sense you, vamps will be flying and omnibusing in from miles around for a suck of you. If I'm allowed to stay I'll make sure your spit levels never drop, so you'll always be ready for them.' His little eyes brightened. 'Why, I could hang upside down from your lapel when you go vampire-hunting!'

'I have no plans to *ever* go vampire-hunting,' I said bitterly.

But stay he did, and it was probably just as well, for he was correct about word spreading among the vampire community of that rarest of delicacies, vamp-tainted human blood, and I had no choice but to defend myself against all comers, at all hours. In the cause of keeping this activity from my parents I took care to pretend that nothing had changed, helping in the shop and delivering the meat every day even though my contaminated blood made me more sensitive to its foulness than ever. Never again was the Count able to change out of his bat form, but he kept his promise to maintain the level of my spit pot – very handy that, for there were a lot of vampires out there, all wanting a drop of me. Singly they came, and in twos and threes and fours, but I soon got the measure of my powers and strengths, and my assailants always suffered worse than I in our encounters. In time I became such a scourge of vampiredom that, when old enough to make decisions without my parents' approval, I changed my name to something rather more heroic than Jerome Ignatius Granville Offal-Trype.

What name?

Well, it seemed only right to pay homage to the great Edric MacIntyre-Quiver, author of the tales of derring-do that so entranced and inspired me in my youth. I borrowed part of his name – the Mac part – and his famous abbreviation – Q – and had visiting cards printed which announced me as...

Jiggy Mac-Q, Esq.

A LITERARY NOTE

There never was a spinner of tales called Edric MacIntyre-Quiver, but there was a writer who published under the pseudonym 'Q'. This was Sir Arthur Quiller-Couch (pronounced 'cooch', not 'couch'), poet, critic and novelist born in Cornwall in 1863. Sir Arthur's surname was a pairing of his grandmother's, Jane Quiller, and his grandfather's, Jonathan Couch.

JIGGY HISTORY

Jiggy Mac-Q fought vampires for many years on the quiet. Count Zornob, in his bat form, stayed with him until the night Jiggy was sharpening some pencils in anticipation of a battle the following day and the Count inadvertently parked his bat-hind on one of the upturned leads, which instantly turned him to squealing dust. Fortunately, Jiggy had built up quite a stock of the Count's spit by this time and was able to continue his work for some years by applying it sparingly to various parts of his body. During these years his father retired and Jiggy exchanged the butcher's shop for a bicycle emporium that specialised in fine iron spokes, a quiver of which he carried at all times for emergencies that had nothing to do with bicycles. In addition to the spokes, few bike sellers can ever have stashed as many sharpened pencils in their pockets as Jiggy Mac-Q.

In 1917 Jiggy met Eliza Dobwalls, a draper's assistant, whom he married a year later. Eliza, for all her charms, could not get over the sheer stupidity of a name like Mac-Q, which she now had to bear, and when she produced a son she dropped the vicar a couple of sovereigns to persuade him to write 'McCue' on the birth certificate instead. Her husband was not pleased when he realised what had been done to his chosen name, but, like most of the males of his line, he quailed before female displeasure and put up with it.

Jiggy and Eliza's son was christened William, and he was the first and possibly last ginger-haired McCue in history. Because of his hair colour, William's unimaginative schoolmates called him 'Ginger', a name that stayed with him into adulthood. In his late twenties Ginger McCue, a restless sort, became an explorer, and in 1947, on a brief return to his homeland, married a childhood sweetheart who, the following year, presented him with a son. A few months after the boy's birth, Ginger, testing a new rifle, accidentally shot himself first in the foot, then (while yelling in agony) the head. He did not survive the second of these errors.

Michael Lawrence

Don't miss the next Jiggy adventure
(in the 17th century!)

MICHAEL LAWRENCE

JIGGY AND THE WITCHFINDER

Jiggy's got some amazing ancestors –
make sure you discover them all...

OUT NOW!

jiggymccue.com   wordybug.com

Read on for an exclusive extract of
Jiggy and the Witchfinder...

AS TOLD BY THE
17TH-CENTURY JiGGY

Great Piddle. What a name for a village. What an
address. And the village down the road is called…

Little Piddle.

The villages are called that because the
neighbourhood river is…

The River Piddle.

Little Piddle is actually bigger than Great Piddle.
I suppose it's called Little because the river gets
really narrow there. The narrow bit feeds into a
pond known as Piddle Pond, which never runs dry.
I mean *never*, even when there's a drought on, like
there was at the time I'm going to tell you about. It
hadn't rained for weeks and the river was

absolutely waterless, but the pond was as full as ever. It's important to know that because of what happened there.

My name's Jidgey O'Dear, but it's not my fault. Jidgey was the name of a very ancient ancestor – a saint, actually – who did some holy stuff in a place I've never been to. It wasn't until I was about ten that my mum discovered that St Jidgey was a sort of nun. Yes, my parents gave me a female nun's name! I ordered them to keep quiet about that unless they wanted me to never speak to them again. My folks aren't like normal people. Even my nan says that, and she's my mother's mother. I'd been sent to stay with Nan in Great Piddle because of the war, which my parents had been fighting in. Their side won, but they hadn't come for me yet because they said there was a lot of clearing up to do, whatever that meant. Nan didn't think much of the war. Said it was just a lot of stupid men with long hair (mostly) fighting stupid men with short hair (mostly). My dad was one of the stupid short-haired ones, and so was Mum, though she wasn't a man. She'd lopped her mop before going off with Dad to fight, but she got really narked when people called her a Roundhead. 'What would you prefer, Squarehead?' Dad asked, and she thumped him. Fierce lady, my mum. You wouldn't want to be on the other side when she came at you waving a sword or firing a musket. Given the chance, my dad would stop for a chat about cloud formations or something, but Mum would have the chatty enemy's head off and stomp it into the mud before he could get any further than 'They say it'll be raining by the end of the aftern—'

Nan's name is Kat Butterby. She's tall and lean like Mum, and her hair's still dark, though it gets a mite haystack-in-a-windish at times because she doesn't bother much about appearances. She has a black cat, which people call Kat's cat, though his actual name is Sly. He's called Sly because from the day he strayed into Nan's life as a young mog he was always sneaking food away when he thought no one was looking. Nan also has a fancy man, Frankie Merk, though he's not really very fancy. Frankie and Nan got together after he came to her for something to cure a wart in a very Merky place. She gave him one of her ointments and he said that if it worked he'd come back and attend to whatever jobs she needed doing about the house. 'Thought that'd be the last I'd see of him,' Nan told me shortly after I went to stay with her, 'but a week later, back he comes, all smiles. "It did the trick!" he says. He was very happy not to have to stand up all the time any more, and he kept his word about doing those jobs. Been here ever since.'

Frankie and Nan seem to like being together even though they're so different. Frankie isn't bold and tough like Nan, and he's shorter than her, and bald apart from a matching pair of side bits, but they laugh a lot together. Nan likes a laugh. She even gave her cottage a name that made her smile. The Hovel, she calls it, though it's nicer than you'd think from the name. The Hovel's garden is full of herbs and things, and one entire corner is given over to itchycoo plants. The itchycoo is well-named because if you crush its pods and rub them on someone's back you can give them a really insane itch. I know this because when I was younger me and my mates did it all the time. Gran doesn't grow itchycoo to make itching powder, though. Quite the opposite. By boiling and treating the pods in a certain way, and adding a handful of secret ingredients, she makes a cream that *cures* itches. All sorts of itches, in all sorts of private nooks and crannies.

It was just as well that Nan knew how to make anti-itch cream because there was an epidemic of itchiness at the time I went to stay with her. The itch didn't get the three of us, but a whole bunch of others were driven crazy by it, and every morning she sent Frankie off with a handcart full of the cream. There were a few other things in the cart, but because this was her most popular product she called him the Itchfinder General. Like I said, Nan had a sense of humour. She only charged for the things she made if her customers had money. If they were skint she did a trade, which meant that she sometimes had more turnips and carrots and eggs than she and Frankie (and me when I stayed with them) could chomp in a month of Mondays. One customer was so grateful to be free of his itch that he gave her half a pig. I felt kind of sorry for the other half. Can't be easy standing on two legs instead of the usual four, or snorting with half a snout.

Life was unbelievably quiet in Great Piddle, and

as there was a shortage of boys my own age to mooch with, I spent most of my days and hours and minutes bored out of my walnut. But one day of early August, with the sun hammering down like it had for weeks, things got a little less quiet, and stayed that way for most of the next day too. It started when Nan sent me to Little Piddle to get some honey from Widow Honey (yes, really).

'Give her this tub of ointment in exchange,' she said.

'Has she got the Itch?' I asked.

'This isn't itchycoo cream. It's for her veronicas.'

'She has more than one daughter called Veronica?'

'Not daughters, verrucas. Foot warts. She calls them veronicas. You'll have to ask for directions when you get to Little Piddle. Honey Cottage isn't easy to find.'

'Will she be expecting me?'

'Yes.'

'How'd you know?'

Nan grinned. 'I'm a witch.'

She often said that when people tried to pin her down about what she knew. Nan knew all sorts of things, and liked to keep most of it to herself.

On the way out I passed Frankie Merk. He was by the gate loading his handcart.

'You been given a job too, Jidg?' he said.

I held up the tub of ointment. 'For Widow Honey's veronicas.'

He smiled. 'Batty old Tilly.'

'Tilly?'

'Widow Honey. She's my cousin.'

'Oh yes?'

'Yes. We don't see a lot of one another, though. It's those damn bees of hers. Not a huge fan of bees, me.'

As I went through the gate I almost tripped over Nan's cat. He'd probably seen me coming and thrown himself across the gate to trip me.

'Hi, Sly, what's a'purring?' I said, jumping over him just in time.

He bared his fangs, like he was saying, 'Touch me, son, and you lose a knuckle.' Sly is not a friendly feline. Not with me anyway.

It was about half a mile to Little Piddle on a twisty dirt road, but it seemed longer on a day that warm. By the time I got there my throat felt like old parchment, so I was pretty keen to find Widow Honey's and beg a drink. I might even have taken a sip of river water if there'd been any. The river ran through the middle of the village but it was so dry now that you could've ignored the two little bridges that crossed it and jumped down and strolled across without so much as a squelch. There was no one about to ask the way to Honey Cottage, but as it turned out I didn't need to look for anyone because someone found me – by tossing a bowlful of water out of a window I was passing beneath.

I glared up through my dripping hair. 'Thank you so much. Just what I needed, day like this.'

'Sorry, didn't see you there,' said the person who'd drenched me. She squinted down at me. 'Do I know you?'

'Only in your dreams,' I snarled, miserably plucking my wetness.

'I only dream good stuff,' she said. 'You look lost.'

'Before, I was lost. Now I'm lost and wet.'

'The sun'll dry you out in no time. Where are you trying to get to?'

'I'm looking for Widow Honey's.'

'Honey Cottage?'

'Yeah.'

'It's not that easy to find,' she said.

'I know, that's why I'm still looking for it. Though I'd much rather be standing here dripping and talking to strangers in upstairs windows.'

'I'll take you there.'

'No, just show me which way to go and I—'

I didn't bother to finish. No point. She'd left the window. She was down right away. When I repeated that all she had to do was show me the way, she said she had nothing better to do in this dead and alive hole, and led me across one of the little bridges over the waterless river. On the opposite bank, she said:

'I'm Dolly Byrd.'

'Sorry to hear that,' I said.

'You?'

'Jidgey O'Dear.'

'Oh dear.'

I sighed. Everyone said that.

At the far end of the village Dolly Byrd showed me to a wall of person-high cow parsley.

'Go through,' she said.

'What?' I said.

'Go through.'

'Why would I do that?'

'Because it's the way to Widow Honey's.'

'It could also be just one step from the edge of a cliff.'

'Bold, aren't you?' she said, and swept the cow parsley aside.

Beyond was a narrow track bordered on both sides by grass too high to see over. I stepped onto the track. Dolly Byrd stepped after me.

'How far?' I asked as we started along it.

'All the way,' she answered.

We walked on in silence. When the silence got really deafening I filled it with another question.

'What happened to Mr Honey?'

'Mr Honey?'

'Widow Honey's husband.'

'There never was a Mr Honey,' said Dolly Byrd.

'There must've been. Why else would she be called Widow Honey?'

'Widow Honey is no more a widow than Honey Cottage is a cottage. She's never been married. Decided when she was about nine that she liked the idea of being a widow, and the name stuck. Some rain'd be nice.'

The sudden change of subject made me miss a step.

'Rain?'

'Specially if it fell on you,' she said.

'Why on me especially?'

'It'd wash off the water I threw over you.'

'Why would it need to? Water's water.'

'Not necessarily.'

'What does that mean?'

'It means the stuff drying on you isn't exactly...'

'Exactly what?'

'Pure.'

'I don't get you.'

'It was from the chamber pot under my bed.'

Don't miss Jiggy McCue's next
adventure in the 17th century!

MICHAEL LAWRENCE

JiGGY AND THE WITCHFINDER

Jiggy's got some amazing ancestors –
make sure you discover them all...

OUT NOW!

jiggymccue.com   wordybug.com